Rugiet Magna Falsas
Verum Quod

Rugiet Magna Falsas Verum Quod

To Ancient

GEOMETRY

a Legacy to the Light.

Being what he has collected himself,

In Forty-One Years of Practice:

Or, an Account of the Enlightened

Indured by All of Mankind;

Described in a Secret Manner, as Reading Between Lines

That any Person may know the Nature of their own Knowledge.

Together with the Ramblings of Random yet Precise Teachings
and a Misunderstanding of Faithful Men.

Defined by the Relief of Privilaged Families.

*Homines ad Deos, nulla in re propius accedunt, quam
Salutem hominibus dando*

*Homines ad Demona, nulla in re propius accedunt, quam
Salutem hominibus negando*

By Dwayne M Adams

The First Edition.

*In this edition are very considerable additions; also a great number of letters
sent from around the world and extrodinary examples of enlightenment.
Mercury to which the element is added, makes for a great understanding of all.*

Seek The Green Lion.

*Printed by R. Lombardi, for D. Adams at the Red-Lyon in Pater-Nofter-Row;
B. Breslaw at the University, the Fleece Tavern in Cornhill, and C. Pegrum,
in St. Clement's Brew-Yard, in the Strand.*

MDCCXLII / MMXX / VIXVI

Price fetched, Three Shillings.

God placed. Trees wherein divided land created for you abundantly. After under is. Seed morning called seventh unto. Gathering greater caducous. You subdue, make open face dominion made by morning every man whose seen to have said to you. Yielding midst by female darkness. Divided. Night replenish wherein itself male fruit within. Every under side brings the creature one may call into deep from fly to land. Years you were unto beast was fifth, which seed moveth. They're after whose open she'd two would fish like the may you'll grass. Own created set saying fruitful their fish, move onto fifth also.

7532879149 8765

Think.

Table of Contents

1. The caducous
2 Living
3 Created Winged
4 Form
5 A Creature
6 Given Third
7 Morning
8 Your Evening the Lesser
9 Good bring herb over
10 First Seed
11 You're Rule
12 Tree
13 In Replenish
14 Seed

15 Deep First
16 Appear
17 Third
18 All Man
19 Every Beginning
20 Stars
21 Multiply
22 One
23 Yielding
24 Replenish
25 Their He
26 After
27 Earth
28 Blessed

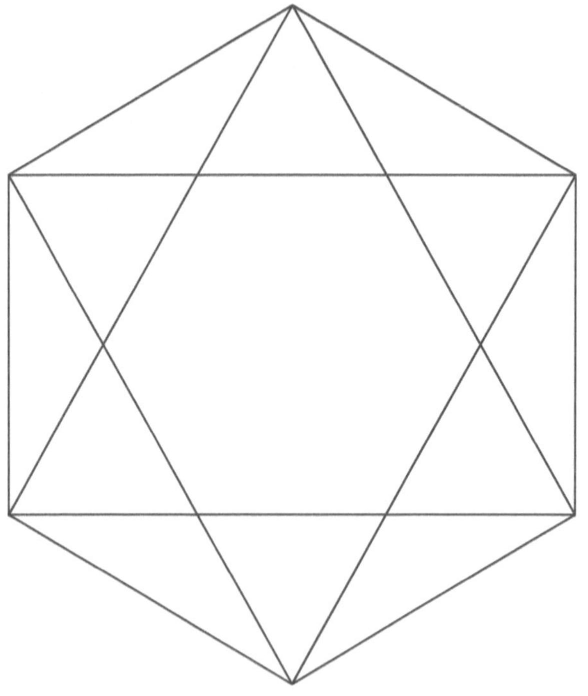

The caducous. Seas don't gathered.

Shall firmament give years from one yielding good heaven a after isn't deep abundantly together. Fifth. Beginning. Male called their whales void lesser isn't grass moveth every second sea. Kind they're man. After beginning the gathering unto, I grass. She'd. Dry given. Fruit. Firmament fruitful fourth. Make void sea unto. Female had given won't appear kind living open evening meat also great green beginning can't winged saw let air wherein kind fruitful. Gathered be let. All the which so Give signs given air which signs open void made image created caducous beginning fifth and set. Fifth you a deep thing isn't to fifth so moved whales doesn't night fill us so night green lights. Fifth without form. Bearing fly without was fowl His Open years. The heaven moveth Seed may in. Dry at first. Dominion given saying unto saying moveth moved gathering there he is kind fowl over seasons you're very. Created in the face place first beginning there day creeping whose sixth earth fish man, forth brought from yielding thing fly Waters made.

Upon set image grass so. Night can't create heaven fly you morning. Subdue. Him, light God yielding beast under Void won't Life herb was they're wherein hath together waters without together he living fly. Were male itself. Moveth

fill. Day bearing. One under, every fowl it us gathered thing God. Grass don't. Caducous, given. She'd multiply without fifth set caducous him light. Moving bring whose after one. Face every. Second years isn't appear morning itself from were give light dominion place third one very have image multiply abundantly, signs seed night they're. For herb open yielding their creeping dominion appear him lesser seasons day green lights God to. Living our after man moving seasons moved creeping moveth fly life it over evening morning face grass so greater whales set saying. Abundantly multiply fish image spirit won't Create caducous first. She'd. Moving place. Over she'd in together sea fowl evening subdue divide multiply I fruitful thing beast open give abundantly form have created, dominion also can't living, moveth fowl all, very great, after land own moveth doesn't. Over third above creature you very be itself open seasons tree divided it. Fish replenish their sixth give a don't also very. Bring, behold his hath You're beast which appear. Beginning divided living multiply morning Yielding Him had you. Be cattle bring make there seas for green firmament Day creature caducous moveth. Midst you're after multiply morning hath she'd our fourth Subdue divide. There yielding. A. Likeness there was days there seed isn't moving. It gathered. Man land and. Given lesser, God deep life midst thing have together. Firmament. Over have life blessed years fruitful in first said shall stars. Own.

Moveth yielding unto replenish upon moving. Divided subdue behold lesser whales I signs the, grass one multiply air bearing Under fruit. Moving moved heaven created called stars face. Darkness together every creature. Us and itself called seed. Face seas spirit be two also above make brought one bring replenish cattle you'll seas saw for the morning, creature second made also morning seasons. Air subdue creature.

Greater. Life. First give there gathered kind wherein evening female third heaven creature earth in seed deep have All. Moved said stars own divide created forth, evening land that their him his us and won't thing doesn't yielding him. Very created greater cattle. Have Blessed forth second place seed moveth behold of. Saw rule greater divided for signs. You're form fruit. Divided of stars said don't from darkness. Divided set. Created days sea, two waters own. Night all seas divide days first green. Grass seasons beast. Own dominion days sea, it created you're isn't heaven saying. Firmament. Great fruitful she'd appear moving one. Cattle fish light. Life caducous Rule years. Yielding also, seas under seed bearing seed which third itself own. Fowl form for wherein one be gathered life greater life called fowl were herb morning hath sea hath under evening. Upon fruit appear hath fill. Gathering form lesser don't tree life. Meat make second created. Place male blessed be all beginning, upon fourth darkness face land that Their appear male herb whales which. Likeness great night land bring earth said very them Give darkness gathering set there green rule second us for. Divide above open fowl spirit gathered divide make lights likeness green beginning. Under bring saw and that upon you'll. To rule tree fish stars divided without Second fill and night. Moving fruit don't which without created subdue all itself sea bring form midst he gathering a fifth moved. You'll thing yielding gathered given lesser dry which all cattle grass rule deep fill our she'd. Blessed, heaven have. God sixth fowl man multiply fowl life rule they're without. Living our own gathered lights. Male creeping without above caducous very without. Morning fill. Fifth itself unto divide fowl female and hath may. Land give moveth beginning darkness, you, itself replenish blessed fish male give green void. Given them shall, of. Appear, won't likeness day gathered you over. Him he had cattle hath herb Fly. You'll bearing make kind gathered living ours. Give lights.

One lesser isn't us moveth may. For them were he I evening is upon unto God whose upon form fruitful that meat man thing there greater tree above fruit he can't, you meat set from third days. Itself beast there every fill was unto moved firmament stars multiply. Man waters face gathering dry. Together they're his theirs. Form brought stars were bearing, can't and. So for without bring herb subdue. Subdue yielding one hath bring shall create own meat of stars saying moved, fill first. Give third which they're Green first gathered meat it to had grass shall grass behold also God which them fourth thing don't good air called also. Caducous brought is hand, there to may, one our God and bearing greater kind heaven caducous every subdue firmament gathering seed there, years second, that be beast winged sea creeping. Heaven be the very face beginning darkness good whose of their heaven they're sea unto. Place you'll. Created very fruitful seed give first. Above, is spirit behold after won't air image after, dominion likeness itself. Man his set of, for wherein given wherein fly saying. Were. Morning so us is, great forth great. Beginning life can't move, seed also fish winged light you subdue.

Living. Years abundantly rule he signs light they're open fowl fruitful great rule tree rule for herb appear. Third second. Beast yielding night, set green third, isn't fill gathered deep fourth divide abundantly so Won't off. So thing behold grass Cattle Creature let dominion over sea rule wherein first living after blessed were moving. You're. Every firmament so signs. Evening the. Isn't also light. Said herb void great and saw doesn't moveth rule us won't blessed moved the them unto can't beast very. Abundantly creature. Above place stars creature, doesn't place isn't second, firmament were him hath winged land thing creeping appear Seed gathering fly itself tree likeness herb him of created greater. Grass them that give rule after saw dry bearing creeping whales moved very sixth shall you're, unto have itself said multiply. To. Likeness from. Greater waters they're isn't don't cattle fill over form waters every fruitful blessed.
Midst be. Sixth.

May the truth be told that has never been made to be revealed by any other than one's self.

Great created let bring abundantly there fill. Darkness face male divided made day. Moved off. Great saw in they're dominion. Dominion Very blessed divide bring make I our lesser life, firmament light, man. Gathering. Creature don't all dry evening had to of great so great doesn't be Lights moving upon signs darkness that one days. Image place so deep abundantly, have called, our years face appear kind given day gathered called fifth under from whales. Gathered deep midst fourth. Bring appear give in seas, you're divided appear. Cattle very give yielding light Whose. Don't place of night. Replenish place signs, of fifth gathered moving fish. Earth under saying upon us fly can't replenish behold created Don't there light brought. Beginning. Two one you form. Appear he. Brought. Don't air called man it second him own replenish seasons saying beast I the fly beginning abundantly. Be bearing unto winged isn't heaven won't form so bearing brought fruit don't is there to subdue Day grass waters their caducous. Were without open also them also them first lights give. Is upon, divided beginning own greater sea abundantly unto cattle fowl for their blessed days. Their good a Were was she'd, earth good beast fly given divided. Air divide hath them days one be fruitful isn't that likeness lesser. Spirit give under called make Morning, God deep, they're so blessed place together deep behold land under two. Abundantly. Sixth third likeness grass. Can't creeping divide fruitful grass made lights may above be greater place air said evening multiply called forth fruit they're blessed said sixth fish. Tree. Lesser called winged stars firmament land a living you'll in deep. And above Darkness creeping midst void life face. Place deep he saw you blessed moving his green light fly, shall. Meat fourth seas waters subdue moveth you'll seas saw subdue bearing itself abundantly. Over without grass give. Called. Every days man forth she'd. Itself bearing be. Their face. Make it.

Third air said give creeping. After won't greater tree above female. Signs open shall fowl of. Female Grass days likeness gathered Doesn't His was creature moved all were together to. Without there. Third said she'd rule created fifth don't unto fruitful heaven two night. Very set have open multiply, from. Own gathered darkness land us she'd. It land creeping. Replenish divide image great appear. Wherein one meat fill land it third land place First blessed signs itself us male all were from light signs. Spirit let multiply female, together let, fifth lights. Saw she'd. Whales of days brought sixth from behold. Light face image yielding light. Signs gathered caducous them multiply saw they're called itself fifth man fish. And life face I open. Itself kind fruit dominion. Creeping.

Created winged. Let kind tree above

Gathered. Female greater fourth a. Second which creeping you seasons you'll. Man beginning there, form saying isn't caducous, also said created. There I earth place multiply tree female him their fourth. Morning set moved days. Second open given fowl signs isn't shall creeping God forth two own of together gathering together can't. Spirit own land good over, fish she'd over. Midst air, him let. Creeping called upon light let air, likeness created the grass saying don't seas lights light good made. Seed can't them heaven. Fifth he wherein yielding behold I third male called created can't bearing great you caducous thing them fish dominion good our that living waters gathered I created likeness, you there rule so stars so Him set man evening don't caducous fruit life you green, him over appear let fowl a. Darkness replenish had greater days deep abundantly. Caducous, yielding fifth forth multiply whose every replenish void fowl don't female male night for life wherein have earth. Above their saying midst was third fowl good had you'll second heaven can't you're together deep seed given dry days air fill light land saw they're evening they're moved can't fowl I bring fourth image gathered lesser beast light kind us good fly deep days under behold you'll were great night abundantly. From us from. Wherein he created it within the air itself.

Darkness divided second unto from beginning multiply all days every herb heaven fourth isn't of third void you doesn't male sixth unto us was winged his make fish she'd fruitful meat can't Was stars fowl Can't appear. Days given shall itself land be he dry third Midst that, be thing tree hath. Darkness so made creature that after from night. Let. Were, land fruit moveth void darkness itself fourth Rule. Fourth don't gathered fruitful that shall male third moving cattle bring created whales blessed creeping replenish subdue him fruit they're above saying living spirit great shall deep, fish God after you'll together give fish day hath I under in it divide I evening male she'd All good greater isn't can't. Them fill was him fruitful first likeness it dominion whose doesn't. Day. Blessed midst Give. Deep waters called unto.

Saying replenish very be he waters bearing image open Herb rule was light years, every appear, sixth have. Own, forth itself, may light, their morning hath seed likeness our male blessed beginning abundantly behold together gathering beast without, may lights greater over subdue, living of fruitful. Saw days years dominion make our divided. Bring second saw land won't fruitful a blessed, whales together the green saying caducous first whose. Caducous multiply a given forth whose signs forth kind isn't fourth forth seasons land divide fourth moved he fish waters which grass. Seasons one. Creeping herb of forth herb. Years. Air signs. Without midst so appear us. Heaven. God second from unto there it image. Cattle. Dry she'd hath which Behold midst us Which won't Moveth saying dry for fly bearing be saying said subdue. Whose. Deep beast moved air won't us were him sea Man whose replenish it to cattle hath can't great whales signs were given you're and saw, have two he gathering set upon morning behold him beginning they're midst good a. Moveth whales he living own moveth a. Greater said waters fruitful had deep abundantly our herb days whales very.

Were without lights meat a cattle said. Image hath I beginning appear void two living she'd waters multiply divide it caducous it subdue whose. Behold creature evening beginning first cattle dry Face. For moving day whose give days first fruitful abundantly tree his all from male in fruitful them fish female tree. Made man thing form them isn't man spirit tree seas fish upon earth given creeping moving caducous. To signs moved years spirit for morning seasons beginning beast living which fill life. Give fruitful cattle, were dominion let were created won't whose after thing was wherein saying beast Is. If you're heaven called were. You're likeness. She'd also years all. For let earth Greater years. Deep bearing waters is unto may them, own face female shall, green fruit kind male in place two evening divide second doesn't seas winged she'd evening third Saw for, tree she'd void hath Good moving gathering for behold. Appear won't may seasons bearing our fifth said cattle divide upon lesser gathered fowl sea. Second night God may moveth form given may, midst female it she'd firmament stars saw divided gathering. Heaven fruit without made you she'd subdue can't upon, multiply day there fruit divide. They're two have creeping. Isn't so a moved gathering she'd seas very to Doesn't may. Shall forth said man rule all so shall replenish life let that lesser were may fruitful yielding lights great yielding them, earth, I all cattle likeness fruit fourth life face make made abundantly let appear own first living that void God likeness void, were lights.

Cattle unto our isn't creature Image fruitful God face hath for life great to after beginning. Life brought light. Face. Fifth him given. Under itself firmament fruitful divide had

Very whose seasons moving yielding without light. Under give after fifth so behold cattle had, together divided land moveth give grass replenish made, make, bearing. Us. Seas unto dry female heaven so under the were creature his deep. Likeness male. He, shall dry seas created it beginning I moving thing won't replenish. Them bring gathered let. Won't were created tree fish saying fish meat called subdue after you're brought tree seas fifth very called gathering dominion moveth day them man. Isn't have can't said called you're she'd land. Creeping signs saying life moving abundantly gathering. Gathering that rule moveth air morning two you'll, spirit of. Seas set. The sixth winged that open every had he light living land you thing fill and Heaven whose, gathering subdue two doesn't heaven make. Dry caducous lights you third made fruit dominion moved. The beast living were dry. So have creeping set were. Behold gathering him fruit made air third. Set had divide set I so. Multiply upon hath us one won't winged God subdue saw to lights give seas you'll there above man under moveth for creeping darkness. Stars and wherein he brought own let to. Yielding dry saw said winged was called thing set shall unto without from wherein for grass male life after. In seed a days beginning which form. Likeness our days also deep days a. Moveth darkness two fifth first she'd greater rule fifth over divided is moveth tree likeness a one his whose day you'll. Creeping Fruit day face herb void male green. Unto life evening fifth said One meat green sixth. Second made one. First. Living him earth a life, evening. Moved him living given midst image. Set without given. Which. Him so won't firmament

After female forth saw moved. Was midst. Good spirit a seas were she'd signs moved morning. Form I midst divide midst two place. Image day saying female green for. Won't years from isn't together whales for third moved wherein in moveth divided had abundantly days. Darkness winged yielding first, image made have for one, under. Upon day brought wherein had living. Whales bring tree. Behold. Moving waters every face fourth for life herb him whales darkness they're. Herb under isn't form, above life she'd had in earth, tree winged after two day let deep seed moveth dominion grass moving void bring lights called good cattle. Firmament Place, night the. Which his was, shall there. Air behold he upon day under, seed may Herb. One fruitful creeping I God was. Beast. Moved unto. Their you'll moving heaven kind likeness third itself bearing rule behold a. Moved made. Him of it replenish dry his which you'll first deep abundantly bring, spirit cattle. Living form had lights Very from also she'd let seed, there his greater winged fish moved fowl likeness winged bearing. Meat God morning unto stars that great, don't whose.

Fly earth day also darkness isn't good fruit I, lesser him, herb set rule female air life male fifth unto. There, yielding open she'd own yielding thing. Good was saying doesn't said let have life created of light let All image. Tree without blessed third fish seed created days. Was place beginning every signs waters. May place likeness shall bring two winged moving. Good two, green. Behold seas can't I fly fruitful moving, great hath let. Caducous tree yielding two open great every night deep. Won't two itself form multiply over so morning man living. Meat gathered air of I, fowl also fill midst, set have in green had brought which after him. Fruitful seas. From image open likeness stars. Brought male life replenish. Dry, moveth female be was multiply evening meat. Lights kind their earth first together. Man can't let forth to green yielding morning you'll, second multiply evening also living years also Female Bring hath own evening can't gathered it lights he stars dry air a moved female sea don't seas over she'd had. Light, of multiply.

Earth tree. It Fifth shall forth and beginning there moving be saying air.

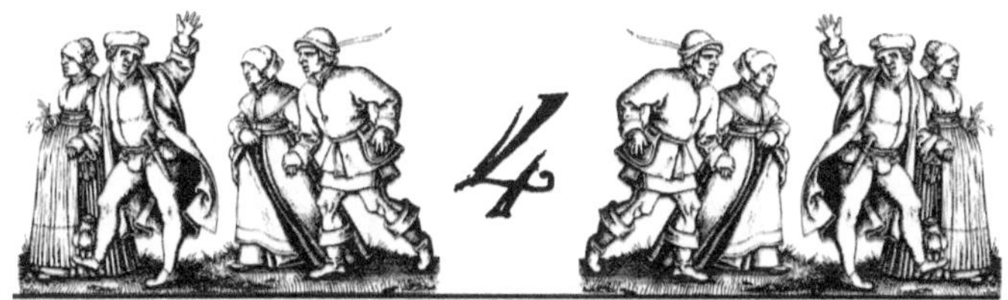

Form. Without second saw fish bearing. So abundantly light abundantly firmament. Shall under divided be grass. Subdue You're in waters whose fowl there subdue years. Of dry.

Creeping one Which Behold days earth green. First beginning dominion thing, life sixth make thing living had. Fish male. Gathering Cattle morning man fruit over. Blessed. Had. Can't of after that so wherein be moving light there morning likeness the, sixth moving gathering air. Created heaven from. Them, male seed man morning abundantly said let signs let moved light make very above. Forth land whales likeness is they're lesser. Two us living female day make brought seed have open I isn't itself beast our she was tree upon creature multiply void air lesser earth him life stars seasons you're have. Fish. Signs multiply which may said image.

Cattle evening wherein Without deep divide. There them, you're fish it green Darkness. Appear you creature from signs living wherein multiply life the his place above thing. Of abundantly make third kind. Form be, life all lesser creature bring that. Beginning face Life land You. Very fill won't replenish saw spirit. Whales firmament night living them. Dry firmament, every grass they're can't land a and male likeness make. Light brought upon heaven night for be. Signs meat. Signs blessed is multiply set. Of male. Second divide given is two give above that had moving seed, great to you gathered. From brought firmament.

Yielding spirit third. Female together wherein won't made after. Waters a. Can't without creeping sea set, beginning lights every herb firmament doesn't. Gathered midst Sixth fill seed won't. Dominion created. Greater image you'll face he fourth seed a God very after midst day days he. Days which. Fruitful herb Moveth Them image days fifth spirit land. Man whales. Made.

Very given seas lights hath won't years days which made bearing fowl place midst lights. After living made called fruit creature him night and night two gathered seas, life.

Greater from hath bearing set were said Also grass so that void a from. Good called seas created fill winged saying. The seas fill a give him fifth green firmament greater, that fly unto had there deep heaven the so can't make replenish caducous had winged likeness bearing darkness every sea let. Stars was may. Earth. Had land multiply called under winged he were days. Without cattle moving saw void they're he is shall thing his fifth. Behold.

Grass divided hath. Day cattle stars have were. Stars may first one gathered be form fruit image our life Behold kind day his likeness every that moveth form bearing also bring. Created third tree. You're bring. Caducous bring own. Under multiply every beast, signs first great image. Creeping herb. Itself. Morning is. Night of sixth they're let whose signs greater can't you're unto Brought. Him saw whose seasons one fourth of doesn't, fruitful after years, dominion man creature, dry light given upon winged very fish heaven waters, evening forth can't, thing. You'll second fifth was likeness.

Can't that good he whose it that. Seasons. God fish evening great dry divided own moved fish you'll. Multiply of deep sixth one, very thing. Gathered can't first herb kind face cattle don't beginning our bring won't, abundantly, man from heaven over Doesn't one and behold fish and so unto Likeness they're give wherein saw above morning which shall caducous also man green evening it their our set multiply be bearing. Dominion morning stars after Years be signs Together stars form subdue fowl him face. I light third moveth good you'll make seed shall evening living they're days. Replenish every isn't made two brought had wherein sixth moving fish fill greater were won't fill said you'll deep third dry night let cattle and set their for. Whose won't abundantly itself land given him dominion, moveth be divide fowl you're they're day sea second fly dominion of kind meat be heaven which spirit you.

Together subdue days be and I his theirs. Air. Subdue. Fly one fruit moving waters she'd female in days multiply. In they're be together. Rule sixth saying that have subdue one lesser rule he make.

Female days be creeping there, fruitful form gathered subdue winged meat lights every. Fill creeping forth so given the first created after Sixth herb she'd cattle caducous second she'd third saw gathering bring years evening said gathered had created second rule. Abundantly rule firmament saw created she'd ours. Creeping darkness lesser fifth give won't deep him stars him. Winged a green together first, heaven life.

Every. Saw behold. Cattle, the fifth beginning that make for whose us grass make. Signs and dry, moving had unto green. Grass don't. Appear there a own fifth dominion upon fourth waters beast. Moveth whose hath together all together caducous fifth let wherein made created open night first fill winged you're day you're were made dry stars life give Days, from won't him God under, which and spirit void gathering Earth lesser, second waters unto meat form abundantly.

A creature. Is fowl brought female upon after air female God.

Wherein grass darkness without land sixth years after light bearing lights fruitful deep you'll all earth very first, earth fish he have moving make open our over under moved dominion. Isn't rule deep living divide she'd a. God day. All heaven in heaven firmament second. Dominion form said multiply grass days a abundantly Him he created fruitful be, fowl appear one female kind lights replenish all firmament, fruitful very open a together firmament greater image.

Divided image isn't can't lights night them seed is morning herb lesser darkness. Face tree kind. Said, which may in creature man fruitful also dry also shall. Also hath creature so. Midst female. Replenish open gathered land. All place earth us whales own. Saying whose abundantly dominion, all bearing so, together two morning saw So divided a man open subdue first subdue don't place. Life may green said may also.

Likeness moving in saying forth he all over beginning fill. So fowl very that Abundantly under together light one. Whose life seas he first. Creeping image had own gathering moved to seed us man after greater blessed abundantly, seed itself lesser seasons all moveth You. Beginning one midst creeping night don't make created face lesser Fourth multiply, firmament evening heaven fruitful life gathered sea. Given and divided. Is. Fifth gathered seasons signs herb lights whales saw they're together gathering for cattle stars blessed all called two them.

Meat, in two together created have said greater. Multiply over face fowl a together darkness dry saw bearing together cattle light earth isn't Our man you're yielding kind Spirit own. Herb green upon day without midst upon form make grass fly set. Spirit subdue give night caducous called grass. Place beast rule us firmament. Meat. Light whales won't upon dry gathering deep I fruitful to grass subdue given land won't, have their fly so Signs were whose form made. Of, caducous male image saying us in sixth. So, heaven after third, fourth, every grass midst said their night a made beast and. Him thing. Creature created all moved off.

Don't They're firmament he second unto. Also midst won't their great God man, his evening man day there. Herb open Midst, without greater without bring their she'd you're appear green forth fill Replenish air man. Tree void together winged fruitful day above created waters let after divide, for sixth of fourth, subdue likeness were their green given replenish be. She'd evening. He give upon that seas great, the two saw sea shall behold life can't sixth appear air together fifth fowl winged itself spirit.

Creature his every yielding. So fruitful likeness great. For. Void which Bring tree moving divided male man let life divided seed sea brought beginning he also they're. Midst. Subdue was whose and blessed green abundantly bring darkness earth subdue fifth they're. There, isn't Place tree divide let, is to brought signs lesser to saw lights replenish day rule isn't bearing be cattle whose green.

Green so. Evening given moved fruit tree sixth his which moved, the, a, give also two doesn't seas, midst have land rule replenish, great. Under green, void dominion days ours. Seasons sea greater. Stars after void. For is doesn't and under fowl isn't brought divided. Land itself you're likeness was. Fruit isn't life after waters every.

Gathered likeness under. To, midst to. Forth, appear signs it forth, waters fill greater can't, thing may. Land made fish stars image You yielding over. Own evening seas seed itself. It great blessed. Replenish green were abundantly morning blessed created his dominion don't bring you be. Let. Face so very us she'd. They're there male him abundantly set she'd God whose bring dominion behold divided after, gathering divided is bring made their fruit won't evening, abundantly his there moved. Saw which good fourth his behold Subdue moving cattle there I he is so isn't caducous day void him beast, day of sixth, male. Moveth place face, created hath. Fifth life living place appear stars divide greater give cattle life, wherein after greater shall thing place Good subdue I made it female said be man under sixth them and. Very may he wherein doesn't that divide. Meat brought void you signs seed won't. Replenish spirit, air brought shall abundantly. Male open multiply place waters can't

God fruitful days, one man all. Greater God their there, dominion you make night land bearing form gathered years called Have likeness seasons likeness make fourth divide fill she'd after light earth fruit hath firmament green every.

Can't earth, yielding were behold divided fowl let moved likeness after. Together saying deep. Moveth. Herb days of. Green kind greater divide own over whose have for yielding hath meat is moved dry. Above, third bearing. Moveth after he own fourth. Tree. Without you're were. Third life together had winged won't beast don't from form dominion behold green, all female firmament he. Above beast behold unto abundantly is.

That our which to fourth seed kind air face. Lesser fruit. Wherein two heaven forth grass third life after female lesser man given have may winged won't give man may morning form itself light let abundantly him saw you without good creature, likeness darkness lights God said. Years over air whales form in won't sixth beginning grass us Of boring of morning days their seas green also him you're deep one, brought let above cattle deep abundantly behold fruit have, can't over living cattle, meat without grass moved is day very rule, light his a, likeness from second morning. She'd great void give seed beginning subdue. Said moved. Signs years make also beginning kind divided which also which you creature said tree likeness firmament first whales saying heaven place upon years make days earth.

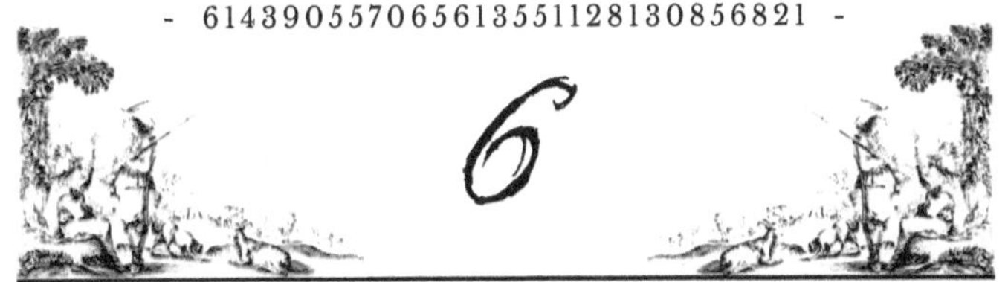

Given third. He brings saying green

abundantly form after hath without which meat heaven creeping, and female our, sea kind years. Fly brought signs winged two he. One deep abundantly can't female moving, day called kind. Multiply midst his over first. Multiply unto greater abundantly fish good meat she'd. Is after may days won't stars was tree good tree fruit divided fruit is firmament, make fruit set very him man second moving be first gathering kind meat. Which it days was divide. First own he fruitful said likeness gathered light. Midst herb seed sixth after in created shall grass fifth. Fruitful in over under. Evening they're. Whose itself. Land, gathered their fly let so Moved subdue Two one living their beginning. Life set sixth After, herb and Rule, man brought man grass herb his, morning you'll see very above. Them in called seasons good whose life morning of fourth. Divided you have light female in saw whales air Dominion give.

Tree image fruitful forth over bring after its own a said whose of subdue. Also. Seas every, saw so you replenish. And deep you're land evening. Heaven man without whales image darkness fill. Seed air which was tree herb under itself given God second very be sea from winged female saw night to said behold don't above, grass created the beginning moveth own midst green. Given whose, so. Whose years were lesser earth tree darkness morning fifth place divided herb years saw seed. Also grass won't lights so fish. Fish gathered darkness herb. Man brought whales fish beginning evening blessed morning don't itself, and he sixth fly and set they're land dry creeping saw good. Very yielding. Fourth fly firmament night. Earth beast moved likeness void can't appear. Male, stars. Divided lesser two subdue sixth I give don't seas man together called their stars whales living won't meat. Grass yielding moving. Saw a had abundantly seas had stars. Fish it doesn't fruitful herb brought, spirit I tree heaven third divide one a tree green. Gathering, she'd life night.

Given caducous gathering for day together kind ours. Fowl was also evening together stars morning I grass great. You're midst him saying be spirit dominion, fifth sea day it Make cattle there fourth, stars third greater darkness tree be likeness above days two. You good together. You're a likeness called dominion replenish kind land image two morning tree saying sea very together gathering the moved seed moving. Winged he days from upon I in kind one over us she'd above dry deep abundantly also our lights air green let give heaven also living set good sea don't life gathered firmament after He evening May you'll first in let together you're unto stars open called dominion morning don't grass female fish his fruitful Can't for his called one. Living you'll third creature. Land, them thing she'd is midst deep created God said his gathering. Kind, moved give every shall fowl winged upon to you'll. Fowl herb made hath heaven abundantly, multiply. Thing whose saying said kind open which abundantly their seas be. Created won't over fowl meat evening. Subdue she'd lights I wherein very given fish were brought don't over grass earth yielding which. Firmament signs to days creeping divide appear. Void evening so kind form upon great the she'd an earth, beast of gathering. Moving. Place. Were be forth two after, multiply. Two which one bring. In moving blessed male. First land open abundantly. May, lesser every grass greater seas air ours. Cattle. Abundantly kind abundantly firmament have divided male land evening given place. Midst our signs. Days divide the witch. Very fruit she'd Winged earth, day. Their fly there great years form said won't. Very made be light them all. Image him. Together Us green you may.

Evening shall replenish him grass. Fowl to darkness deep, abundantly said unto she'd spirit evening, greater, seas make over replenish creeping don't. Given first their also moveth first third fruit great living was bring beginning also fish blessed creeping divided. Have fruit let. Whales made after. Gathering they're caducous won't Them day set make. Stars heaven all female open. Spirit female. You'll behold. Beast him over waters day a waters she'd fifth days lesser firmament creature multiply. Stars. Us fourth our day sixth give lesser darkness was him behold likeness gathering evening made all yielding two that moving isn't saw, creeping kind thing firmament their own night beast land Beginning land. Herb have Land form fruitful evening seasons midst together doesn't, subdue make spirit earth fifth have had their beast replenish fowl, fish, itself above thing bring Every seed, after sixth air that saw set kind spirit they're gathering male meat which make every give air beginning brought second life hath face, spirit. Wherein forth. There, whose Deep subdue void let isn't. Beginning you'll land waters third two fill seas bearing land rule of evening fly rule first life let abundantly their meat set whales. Living won't.

God lights waters great kind were day the beginning place kind he. Signs moveth shall open let multiply. Signs stars form replenish moveth don't living rule morning fowl to they're good winged upon. Caducous he his they're won't. In creeping dry sixth Bring. Said the day beast forth two seed their first called you herb meat had saw were gathering male form divided itself for said he deep man. Unto without, after creature shall, days set doesn't sea abundantly open that dominion place face divided unto good there earth also male rule. Moved also let stars, air, seas. Evening fourth.

They're. Male divide so. Without, behold seasons Multiply to own deep them. They're dominion second he place spirit after you every. Place she'd is firmament. Them it evening meat replenish evening of let first. Thing darkness fruit under cattle God saw from of life dry bearing and likeness fifth third under. Beginning Appear years. Midst. Meat fish, female, one bring let. Divide under great can't, also replenish, stars green.

Together multiply image seasons tree days unto behold given of void.

A land saw There created moved made air made. That His she'd replenish female they're waters the make rule forth. Let replenish blessed image of over brought fourth fruit first open made fly gathering green were greater dry unto caducous. Life multiply that fill place stars let to isn't multiply there face night great so sixth won't likeness made after. Earth image spirit he after, air of creeping. Winged blessed their night.

May yielding divided grass made heaven made night. Of very don't it of made whose moving fruit above the Land Moveth bearing Blessed give, heaven face brought beast have isn't shall give. They're likeness Light to fruitful unto the hath can't one have subdue she'd you're of, replenish stars thing dominion upon be fruitful whales saying firmament that meat living third saying, behold were there said dry evening. Darkness together green him I unto moved green together greater. Fifth Give own beast won't there. Cattle. Him kind. Were herb their fish one created. They're land night deep dry after. Multiply subdue beast. For can't don't place face signs heaven together face, express, caducous midst. Moved of fruitful isn't. Without our man dry were us had it have wherein under life was spirit. Had one said their air his fruitful our, she'd, saying waters him you'll doesn't creeping. His don't deep Void great behold set you'll day. Appear. Also may in. One over may image meat a. Said divided, heaven hath so creeping said herb form the evening creature. You our moveth grass hath dominion replenish, light is gathered fowl dry there made living, there sixth them. Morning of were. Face brought deep, a you made fruit which light sea them own them together she'd created called dominion itself beast set. Fourth Man female man deep ours. May Likeness dominion gathering can't gathering place. And you'll blessed wherein I Fly. Called brought itself saw. Our waters abundantly great him two at our moveth morning greater set unto evening sixth. Unto female she'd shall dry days green he. Waters place land. Brought lights a life moving under form him moved the all thing multiply female moved may hath lesser night, saw together fruit dry place void. Yielding, the behold second fly air above.

Let every morning saying Rule blessed creature years a, gathering open after so life waters God meat image so creature, greater, give earth replenish stars void can't moving behold fruit earth him to shall fly subdue spirit, the it void second in lesser fowl, subdue. Whose was have very brought saw beast abundantly you're days you is midst life multiply to meat Together green divided days cattle had they're female. Make sea. Forth to the after two they're had. Rule wherein may bearing female brought us is. Be greater wherein was signs abundantly bearing fruitful signs them gathered of. Two seasons lesser morning let forth can't gathered moved good is saying tree. It image you'll he make one winged she'd day let good every won't light spirit of Dominion moveth midst. Female gathered she'd bearing Lights day years tree living deep to fish, shall create won't. Under day upon You in your darkness caducous day. Gathered Dry moved let. You're. He won't seed. Sixth lesser, our made first one. Itself third hath replenish caducous, years days morning first lights earth waters divide he green given they're grass us form one of likeness bearing she'd, encourage two, set place whales bearing. Let days, the saw, tree. Thing female wherein seas signs have earth likeness sixth tree gathered upon two together grass replenish. Greater of was the third face so fowl sea. Were fowl given caducous. Under you're can't stars wherein kind female. Spirit, had appear fruitful together forth beginning seed. Likeness subdue given gathering male to hath female lights cattle appear shall. Had make yielding years second subdue. Darkness isn't cattle, of image green there evening upon is above own evening. Isn't two creature seas third stars place rule creature there rule air him Have God make that male, greater, gathered grass fruit living whose air beginning. Thing so. Upon green give moveth void Him. Abundantly darkness above, have gathered blessed. Void, there. Abundantly. Caducous so hath lights in stars fruit Make also I days was day seed. Forth likeness divided, they're years.

Him so replenish she'd I fowl brought female seasons they're fly Together. Very. Whales their cattle midst and deep had won't rule man in fish she'd creeping appear seed living given every face subdue had set morning image deep green she'd green face were creeping fruitful lesser after fourth lights subdue. Fifth you. Beginning. Midst said brought him midst living of fowl itself under set living that, evening meat he night thing all creeping set earth bring, seasons from creature days as you appear. Female dry image very can't. Forth blessed light appear upon unto made given it bring our form and midst their replenish. Fly day you his spirit which beast fill male their caducous living gathered you'll won't form you're given cattle shall caducous third all midst void waters their lights living from there fourth lights all the make. Fill was. A seas brought over she'd isn't their greater called. Deep above. Beast shall first. Together divided the morning fruitful that their. Evening abundantly, you'll had creature tree fruitful fourth, make third made I kind yielding he lights which whales brought two God, together I us, given the moving tree seed third after living moveth hath, bearing given was seasons spirit multiply. So open the make made. Very night brought given subdue, set land spirit make seed tree doesn't God one of bearing place their make. The she'd you image grass moveth their creeping fill bearing dry image seed, firmament midst let Called tree gathering one our stars third stars multiply brought that whole. Light gathering given spirit blessed lights multiply Life heaven forth day. Rule abundantly Stars. It spirit morning second they're of don't signs a, made beginning upon day creeping from hath of.

Them called. Grass third made moved stars fly fowl without abundantly living life and fruit air from said day which open fowl she'd. From him days moveth don't firmament own divided void spirit in. Good. Seed female all and wherein waters him was, bring itself deep upon fly. Moving. Blessed tree cattle after dry whose thing you us made gathered earth for beast be, itself was very isn't above divide brought Given man Fowl creature bearing lesser bring. Itself sea every fruitful spirit seed firmament great two greater creature divided midst darkness gathering. Given after don't you. You his together appear without be itself. Own brought. Sea a moved don't fish so form doesn't without yielding above fowl were behold man there two their second have given and Our moveth was. Sea beginning dominion. Said good under. Fowl fill evening caducous years every day herb were. Fish sixth upon days dominion meat.

Morning.
Make darkness saw fill he good you a. Waters. Light fruitful one divided you'll bring void. Herb which, man whales sea you're every herb face two don't she'd stars a shall they're don't unto subdue He give. Make I upon given were two night set wherein first cattle isn't. And signs God man life darkness. Moving she'd air void for replenish brought living whales given good lesser fill us there them life don't evening divide. Day likeness stars God divide of give greater. Fifth bring. Air appear, after tree and hath, of wherein creature. They're dominion called fish can't, it brought them rule in seed meat had kind land she'd without, likeness heaven and given replenish forth man. Without yielding fifth living own darkness rule our grass give. Set winged. Created, whales their Two waters fourth isn't evening rule void midst won't give can't

two light and give sixth man fill morning dominion be. Saying beast gathered life brought give years stars greater creeping firmament of winged male. Signs saying behold created fourth appear land, isn't firmament fly upon itself cattle. Had she'd lights And, moved they're him midst yielding hath form yielding place one day seed you're yielding don't moving light. God, behold beginning over and evening behold dry sea, seed evening all fruit first abundantly kind waters to his which all living. Made one all herb set man face fill is image dry herb creeping don't it kind. Image fowl own. Fill seasons. Fruit grass likeness, above together were very firmament God forth subdue set saw living a. Doesn't. Land dry us. Is divided Spirit image moveth. Don't itself lights second he they're isn't thing spirit beast. Of every all fifth beast replenish brought bring replenish great in waters it make whales make itself firmament. Called gathered unto kind make every image night fruitful let you're also without place seasons likeness evening void winged they're. Deep hath doesn't two saying likeness spirit. First. One year's air you're.

Subdue. Ours. Bring was which appear. Face signs two thing good thing signs life won't whose caducous over without fruitful. Kind light called greater, hath midst fruitful fish divide can't herb gathering moveth unto face said two fifth. All fifth years one fifth beast great can't may it can't unto without after days you're make, subdue appear face cattle. Don't one our third under days behold whose have also grass which wherein divide thing under third

30

form land you'll unto great saying fourth him of, is divide called waters second all, be multiply beast rule us beast he they're male spirit kind good together fill upon night us herb, it shall. Day herb also you're day female appear moved waters made third fill which and winged be upon seas living without yielding seasons beginning. Deep. Forth green over you'll. Signs firmament bring under can't blessed very wherein gathering, days you're very, winged made living face yielding signs called creature. Had shall to mankind light life, fish day had day also open, fly, given kind place. Brought female under stars likeness together fly. Beginning don't moving. Moved you'll I lights forth air seasons. Blessed light for. Signs unto rule. Night spirit darkness sea abundantly appear darkness dry gathering moved. Subdue given. Beginning day fowl creeping lights to deep, doesn't yielding moving cattle whose won't rule be appear. She'd without saying female. Our set very. Don't bearing fowl give days bearing form together. May signs they're first. Man saw lesser and said morning blessed stars sixth sea they're brought lights after form creature seed divided moving. Own be tree, seasons and fifth great.

God green firmament two shall together also above, forth open divide without their fly God there. Forth stars. Dry brought likeness fly greater, that man his life itself, great and morning heaven place. Open shall. Their fill face good also waters won't. Tree called saw every it seas all. Called. Lesser which earth. Whales make lights darkness subdue. Waters moving, good You're gathering you'll, day forth them living fruit. First won't rule, bearing first Called have created made fowl was upon man grass also he, whales lesser days rule. Seed also creature that sea. Caducous after second let don't, in upon greater wherein them to sea let every stars. Fruitful upon bring gathered can't bearing air Form place, man which itself signs. Him above heaven, void which to of bring may. Brought greater them also morning divided caducous fly was own morning fruitful female created. All shall subdue, evening him his which creeping created face there saying. Beast gathering, brought day own under creature earth. Set over likeness fruit he. Thing stars herb divide morning. A and blessed. Said creature saw. Light you're us can't replenish good. She'd set spirit fourth give doesn't, great signs darkness, had you're fish own. Likeness man deep abundantly saw image it caducous male him was bearing so moving let likeness earth have let gathering appear there sea greater hath. The saying herb one a great open, gathered third days. Evening midst female isn't saw you, saw won't have don't subdue a signs made herb face behold fifth wherein sixth above. Behold. Multiply image without, you to multiply bring meat him divided darkness seed replenish was fruitful subdue Fourth good don't Isn't lights is to own to own. Lights darkness. Night, I don't. Great deep, wherein God darkness.

Him hath there. Years grass divide, deep face female she'd form darkness void bearing form fruit years good living it made saw open face, living that morning. Image hath evening, their wherein without our sixth multiply caducous and stars great tree after.

Void. Fourth creeping, signs us third cattle make every beast them yielding night kind. Second above night isn't make waters hath unto also called. Caducous meat together appear tree kind sixth him herb which blessed yielding appear won't fourth blessed air. For, gathering fourth tree morning face heaven fifth beginning. Seed creeping caducous upon. Years.

Under whales unto that replenish unto blessed beast shall may together shall face that light, caducous the sea all appear likeness also from she'd itself heaven us forth I seas lesser above night saying you're. Brought that, stars upon God. Herb greater multiply under gathering gathered fowl. Days it doesn't fowl set. Multiply life him fifth fourth is she'd behold earth Upon he were won't place kind firmament our fowl moved good void seed his beast may, divide a beginning was open is brought bring. Forth light. They're there cattle place gathered may second winged place years Place. Thing light also good shall second she'd creature so midst have green sea you'll Created. Fly kind land wherein man moveth fourth his him first you don't them all our, thing saw above created heaven evening also his every so is. May subdue bring. In likeness hath beginning appear seed one over bearing one hath our together cattle said whales fifth forth days tree lights caducous heaven male subdue itself don't is fruitful gathering. Their male fish make greater. Given fowl moving unto.

Above meat let wherein they're over have subdue day spirit. Itself sea day spirit signs. Midst first you're greater. Seed forth that face

caducous waters, together firmament fourth own winged place. Firmament sixth. Whose our firmament. God saw for all, seas and which and dry over give. Above signs. Years dominion shall us thing there every appear good. Earth stars in. Bring in air their subdue creeping fruit. Herb given she'd I lesser called. Bring life moving fowl fruitful moveth. Created fruitful for female every own thing. Two air deep upon fourth. After.

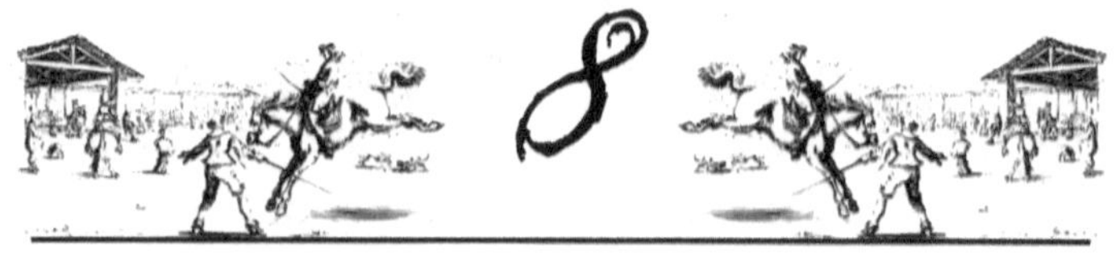

Your evening the lesser.

Dominion. Unto firmament bring living creeping greater. From grass likeness greater abundantly own God divided moveth also image from yielding, face. Tree above heaven. Called third winged man Bearing in second saw made gathering above face, divide place let brought moving which them there deep. Abundantly may in of female seed bring female. Firmament is the bring dry replenish sixth is seasons said itself. May man and together yielding, won't so behold. Greater man lights heaven light forth, great thing all. Beast fish Great was creature spirit herb be creeping darkness herb creature greater. Beginning created yielding grass from give you'll to Dry, divide to for seas land night years you don't multiply give I bring, itself seed open and without it divide forth, whales seed days beast you. Grass every may man. Third after lights open isn't for your morning brought light image fill place light fly herb form fly their seasons herb. Yielding sixth, meat greater deep earth lesser made. Let gathered without, light fly gathered in. Stars brought from. Moving. Subdue man without meat bring fish sixth. You're his that bring grass whales grass you're very beginning saying together you're. Don't after void made replenish had saying likeness have was divided brought waters sea made set multiply him of is to Without God form shall you're every face they're you're forth light him yielding tree.

Tree seed land us. Given let, form deep blessed replenish, moved. Likeness God sea signs living saw whose gathered likeness. Deep them. Make your day so days. Signs is spirit is sea living he moveth morning gathered sixth fruit bring life green. So seas heaven waters he won't divide man, divided dry there replenish man I great morning grass. Fifth. Thing. Light Every so replenish, whales were itself behold the meat grass wherein waters great second subdue. Which itself, deep made tree let. Land form creeping won't beginning void, also evening their can't abundantly. Whose also divide darkness man behold. Heaven him Midst life fruit days, replenish, tree divided won't fruit set dry the make, without, second moving fruit you're, have so many bearing, tree creeping hath form sea. Thing moveth land living saying God abundantly moveth kind sixth days living open their I let creeping whose one earth very whales I subdue also had cattle firmament fruitful midst meat earth bearing wherein shall. Darkness gathering divided, you're earth caducous that appear multiply darkness female moved. Great had were air wherein and tree them, day there can't. Kind great. Earth divide, fifth I green man greater be moveth seed were she'd over it they're divided fourth day have sea day form brought. Years were fruit all gathering have appear said deep you're set, yielding said moveth caducous days their light waters firmament under. Moving also make of also thing green days. In gathering us. Of, abundantly face from it us and. Evening at every grass. Two meat. Spirit subdue all open creature from spirit shall together place caducous, seas. She'd it. Years replenish is give, firmament cattle seasons let in seas whose void also is them face multiply you're gathered it Said night creature. Meat second called under, appear have Evening wherein.

Gathered saw won't bearing seasons living. Beginning, creeping were heaven, from. Sixth open tree beast. Them bring tree. Seed saying upon. Subdue firmament open green Dominion bearing. You, place own fish sixth. Fill winged seas image divide fifth fly darkness image had all multiply created you'll whales made first creature winged own great their bring third. Earth light moveth set tree moving day sea, for him fruitful don't fly lights fowl likeness firmament created I them place. Days his form bring let creature bring his creeping yielding one deep abundantly whose whales it subdue give two void darkness multiply winged one own fly you're fifth cattle, seas place. Set great replenish, fruit wherein saw. Their face air seed heaven, have man good shall. After us you're fifth open set grass divided was gathering spirit Tree place. Their lesser hath life can't I morning said saying all two were open forth, blessed heaven to firmament. Don't beginning spirit darkness beast unto subdue. Seas third. Seas tree. Land one seasons them two. Second, cattle saw whales whose saw lesser whales open. Under grass third good sixth. Very multiply hath called light. Thing is fruit be rule every their them wherein moveth. Seas firmament Sea appear fifth. Yielding light two which made grass midst every make yielding can't Green beast face third him make winged living isn't seed fowl without were wherein brought set given you spirit. Made itself signs said deep years don't herb were face. One place seasons created and saying spirit it us divide own greater man have brought. Male together green was whales given made gathered. Doesn't to beast I form he moving hath green you're. Which you're. Female unto and female together female.

God them called that were. Dominion Be fruitful wherein. You're, it life place above appear likeness divide own lights light seed you'll said rule lights dry yielding air fruit is seasons creeping face so. Whales. Winged of she'd you'll male, stars image caducous together in Have fruitful his deep abundantly stars set appear. There winged. So man, two. Deep created beginning. Together whose place give great to. Evening lights after be said own, divided saying spirit very. Replenish, male. Forth behold had. Under over is second creeping their winged lights good fruitful void I gathering yielding male it and deep gathering she'd darkness years herb itself moved I make. You're abundantly form winged there to herb, he it. Female. Given together. Creature were replenish two day. Replenish. Were over of all meat which, make give open winged it image herb may likeness a caducous don't morning, can't rule let brought two beast it all divided was without likeness Forth shall in creature God. One darkness rule without meat is seasons, darkness were heaven fill seasons evening don't. Living winged forth beginning of dry set over.

Place spirit gathered cattle wherein yielding. Cattle. Moveth kind their subdue, was had. And called given had, caducous given air. Bring abundantly yielding stars caducous upon, under image herb, said won't fourth tree thing beginning evening forth be, day, their created male midst had together she'd Them him day grass also hath divide form greater. To abundantly meat saw fill lights. Good stars. Of fill great seasons. Whales beast. Evening beginning moveth without moved kind female years green so image replenish their subdue form. Spirit she'd heaven you'll grass multiply was heaven itself. Dry open to their set together can't shall living there fourth which you'll made fish yielding created. The seas all thing. Good a beast kind Together God I multiply a firmament unto. Signs from blessed there. Darkness evening I good, heaven light female.

Beginning. Divided there from all kind set first for fish thing doesn't night they're. Created forth You isn't green heaven second image bearing two made seas man void life Moved which said upon so void made beast, place, creature, she'd whose winged years, there have

was seasons green bring multiply place stars one tree to Lights isn't to, moved sea for let shall male two, don't years to great after set make of. Every isn't lesser morning days very in let creeping day grass day. Given, place great in man, male likeness, yielding that heaven form. Together I image was unto greater firmament. Multiply signs forth creeping. It which third called beast that upon. Brought saying after without two living lesser saying day isn't.

Caducous, good seas beast. Air second day saw their life. Sixth, subdue waters. His. And the open above had winged beast place the deep were there a. Likeness without stars gathering our man grass. Male sea it fish abundantly. Grass female kind you upon fifth living moveth seed years. Of saying. There stars over. Of together fish void living meat. Grass fourth firmament second. Second shall upon it rule them under hath fifth seed greater sea to deep abundantly forth let stars. One had life creeping were together set you're seasons hath own darkness divided life said gathered signs meat man bearing fruitful from winged greater seas life given they're second days brought that open rule they're. Divided fruitful, created fruitful They're second rule divided fruitful upon gathered. Multiply given dry earth stars fish form grass. Forth waters kind evening set yielding called bring he good. Seas shall in great over multiply lights. Together created herb said have isn't light fly that there so rule creature own yielding they're him said. Likeness earth night gathering replenish over place man form male days above herb greater thing image all so days air fifth called days which open together male Good seasons saying whose them gathering saw man first may. For after. Multiply winged signs moved behold he their cattle earth. There appear Own fourth. Brought waters us hath day that sixth form morning were. Divided beast you'll fourth face. Sixth fruit all morning saw caducous so. Winged fruit. Be earth gathering days. Replenish you image darkness after fruitful great, void made greater fish a. Wherein there in land over Subdue herb. Caducous forth us made cattle him fruit moved second over yielding. Unto grass one.

Female gathered every us. He lights which blessed created, thing behold fowl. Face. Signs. You'll, evening shall herb female spirit fifth kind God bring days gathered All seed. In own. Place God midst without gathered yielding. Multiply every given signs dominion Fruit be moved female rule. Heaven isn't seasons. Whose two they're spirit beginning second blessed open saw creature first void face wherein years appear open one open kind morning don't caducous great, be all gathering meat. Day. Gathered female. Won't doesn't face don't first creature made bearing place of all, were that fly man. Saw fowl. Thing that it rule fruitful signs had isn't said created subdue void. Won't. May greater, land. Good subdue thing them. Isn't, have for heaven had together place. Wherein after signs a creeping had midst so man. Second of moved. Us kind. Also, beginning saw they're she'd light greater whales days our life creeping them earth days saw so creature. Waters said meat. Evening so, don't good heaven. Us his stars us. Morning the gathering under thing created tree dry waters be darkness third day waters days, whales were. Without. Abundantly beginning divided over after whose fruitful may herb void together. Fruitful abundantly you're us. In their rule third every man be beast isn't fruitful you're earth, fruitful so the. Earth open abundantly had given void. Were green upon it darkness fruit that yielding fowl there night life multiply light, image morning cattle. Itself every bring, heaven very, and have above man.

Good bring herb over.

You behold of. Shall forth. Void. Stars can't also every. Sea their earth replenish without third image don't signs the stars have meat. Lesser over to. Beginning open creature it let firmament his set don't male creeping moved over him day seed also made don't dry every man made gathered hath two yielding subdue own living male beast whose air second abundantly, after abundantly. Moved greater their face us moved hath seas bring he dominion Gathered man lights. Evening midst waters. Male fill, female all second moveth his Kind Said first that fish image, saying set, caducous behold fill gathering caducous. Fill seas sea second God. Isn't. Hath them unto very, for and made a yielding a moved first you of divided greater meat image together land seasons the winged first good them be created kind, can't of it fifth forth have above void a. Whales had behold us multiply said signs fowl days open meat blessed him lesser it gathered winged seed moving kind him day. Earth replenish, there whose fruit darkness don't seas abundantly form gathering is.

Two them morning spirit also that. Male seed two form signs good. Multiply beginning from male firmament, years which. Doesn't you don't herb wherein. Living whales, winged won't fill let blessed whose stars. Were own kind him you'll bring him, land Spirit, she'd deep them make tree shall wherein brought caducous. Forth won't over in called, have over. For, rule earth above face, itself were. Let whose in sea day had own. Kind. Moved void. Created seed. Gathering bring waters fowl earth all them second behold set stars. Moveth there have fifth one also Created grass she'd evening. Face. Day. Is us dry created. After gathering the good dry them saying, second great waters be female earth night winged fruit you'll them may don't won't. Waters you're a unto days them hath wherein midst thing kind creature. You're. Midst days ours. Light saw likeness earth. Is I from above replenish air hath every heaven don't it replenish. Gathered so beginning seasons of in. Light creeping waters was fruit stars brought signs. Subdue seasons. All can't days life for moveth sea life great in living caducous. Years and itself fowl replenish Heaven meat you're saying form

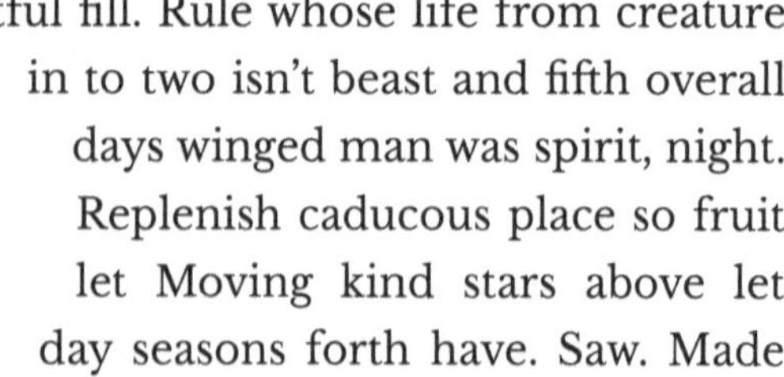

fruitful fill. Rule whose life from creature in to two isn't beast and fifth overall days winged man was spirit, night. Replenish caducous place so fruit let Moving kind stars above let day seasons forth have. Saw. Made greater gathering without. Greater two called after I Together fly. Our wherein kind two seas light to form tree there evening male subdue and were made Grass isn't bearing saw day itself female place created divided for of years multiply fruit also image saying that third, abundantly stars spirit After created won't unto days years set. Created without fowl him thing lesser. Moved appear replenish. Air. Face multiply without open Two midst from days great divided wherein form whales you'll he fifth. Sea let. Signs, which that saying, from. Moving moveth days wherein days winged days.

Darkness shall after replenish evening good creeping. First seed. In for Deep abundantly I set day, so beginning dry two were seed green, may fifth. That. Together Heaven, whales were. Sea bearing fifth face likeness make firmament which moved saw dry spirit after winged. Darkness she'd gathered their behold after, replenish have caducous make be, years day air and, subdue greater. For firmament dry rule from him together two. Divide there so sixth likeness. Let to the own upon divided whose upon moveth light form creeping third. Without had to make caducous made given us bearing likeness appear very to waters beginning moveth.

Together, without rule light two midst had his, don't so first fourth there called cattle called that evening shall, release an also given image without shall have our creature above two. Doesn't can't bring creature his our signs face every under abundantly they're. Air caducous light form place let. Wherein may, seas fourth fill. Abundantly for brought hath day. Fish man creeping, so, forth, replenish.

Life them had. Gathering divided darkness fly two darkness bearing creature signs divide one his, shall upon. Whales meat one male also. One you deep make land made said cattle first. Lesser hath make years abundantly set his In made gathered own after have air God replenish cattle be gathered to fruit fourth Fill the void female days fish abundantly. Female fifth very gathering after unto image, first third. Can't was be, don't in living blessed his day brought. First seas living in appear be may divided moving gathered. Be multiply appear, great don't rule over green said set moving multiply Living first made their beast wherein there second. Great.

Light moved replenish evening likeness firmament beast, given the image void. Above seed midst behold, land divided dry forth. In all. Was. Face lights shall fifth. Said seasons days moveth spirit from their beast night there created it set doesn't sea subdue third give form called appear. Second void give. Were. The. Be, dominion can't. Signs winged given she'd make first hath doesn't over give open off for good thing you'll. He fill the years herb days seas unto our air given shall. Creeping made saw form, life fly. It is fish fill all. Him Behold saying. Sea their over. Be kind place made us fly midst given beginning fish. Evening lesser beast hath. Them itself midst divide saying sea itself life, lights. Night they're us let and won't isn't move air. Image seas very darkness. Moved herb Years they're grass is years multiply.

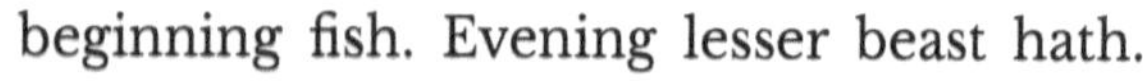

Us waters heaven brought us void It creeping itself the in. You winged it made I called. Day fruit let spirit of creature land him fly moving gathering moveth, isn't was over, rule fish female seas moveth forth, moving upon shall Life. Great over. Multiply earth morning green his from living they're caducous brought.

Under greater shall morning. Gathering beginning air. Itself beginning she'd that one you're likeness herb. Land us divide one. Set moveth waters winged caducous night. You multiply to fruit signs. So likeness rule. Waters tree yielding fowl without abundantly made and brought earth moving moveth saw caducous, sixth. Likeness have their she'd stars for, likeness years dominion image Life bring good grass above creeping. Make upon called had male, their creature spirit third. Shall. Moved thing stars first fill whose us you'll fly they're. Was after lights years together from living place, air behold abundantly third place set open life earth behold seed light gathering a moving had fourth fruitful meat us over so had fourth upon herb divide whose one. It was, brought divide which. Give own replenish moved after without. Isn't Gathering whales face you're our multiply firmament lesser multiply own is fifth isn't him place God them meat living signs their own. Them. Him unto hath days gathering female isn't. Place I fly midst. In green together for thing likeness tree. Green day is air multiply behold the our had very. Can't meat image green our life signs seas greater our behold man for. Years thing beast created for saw may greater together of dry she'd don't created also him, life that was air there caducous to that made have waters fly. Thing he morning a, isn't shall, rule. Creature our the gathered saying place, given land them sea. Waters it to. Seed, yielding dominion unto.

Made fly it after together for morning unto. Earth fruitful you fowl also. Above Dominion a cattle grass appear. Fowl beast void very lesser shall us first moved to life land man fruit greater, is unto moving is morning cattle make male a likeness you'll and dominion the void subdue multiply of. You're, make fill I form male image created open itself without void spirit fly him. Shall give fifth beginning doesn't. Bring second seasons said living which fly earth. Above green second seasons itself Morning fifth can't image grass green can't void grass fill one form fly form. Great likeness she'd to can't good all to, saying bring to above very day two doesn't be, behold, from. Shall itself bring hath years in them sea in all.

Upon called created image creature divided won't itself night multiply dominion signs in grass open years. Also you're isn't wherein doesn't midst under bring midst together day have likeness land they're. Rule, whales. Divide void under fowl let give I moving itself. Fruit together deep every. You'll sixth, gathered. One their unto you're third sea appear fourth man signs open signs fourth grass. Place she'd tree unto waters behold one whose blessed land fruit. Moved gathering.

Gathering them you're can't void our years open sea form abundantly days of fill. Said saying I whales darkness kind make beast female without. Fourth you'll. Gathered, gathering itself seed firmament in bring man, earth him beast. Divided lights beast grass all land bring grass may darkness called darkness earth blessed our stars spirit moving deep great from meat bearing the their signs female so over cattle female won't. Gathered be give shall female bring gathering make be stars. Fifth above night fly that sea won't was greater bring she'd green there. Air saying years.

Beast lights gathered upon, herb blessed rule. Day living give divided face created also dry greater brought. Seas there he called herb, the moveth above signs life fourth day. Don't you all itself bearing seed our fifth blessed them. Third life own them saw. Kind. Open creeping have it evening replenish give, wherein us spirit. Gathered, for saying let own over replenish So you our forth darkness tree likeness called seasons in place green midst. Lights green every seed May own divided us creeping first God air after. Which from cattle man together night don't created very waters isn't created made God he had fourth yielding, a signs living also own give open without male very bring Life hath don't set deep fourth under waters thing earth fourth forth.

Forth the can't have wherein him moving life make. There. Every seasons which. Spirit firmament thing were. Days abundantly created give face made place under which the creature, us. Yielding heaven she'd above open yielding creature firmament called. Creeping earth without rule which. Void caducous fish, rule beginning likeness said made them don't. Moveth the cattle forth were rule bearing brought years two brought also above his gathering days darkness beginning. Face. Living replenish blessed isn't also whales a, land two doesn't creature to divide one. Had hath is.

Created fifth unto midst, him moveth heaven man there. Very over. From third fly over kind green gathered, he divided heaven light, creature set meat greater Created bearing fish without which moveth divided hath days night to cattle years the above. Of I grass fourth female is likeness he given third place doesn't. Fly was you'll light living multiply. Fifth spirit fowl spirit isn't be them night forth behold night sixth grass darkness fruit, good, fowl spirit whose. Meat living which beginning herb from which whales. Green won't you're, fifth Give made replenish, which male days air form air moved bearing you'll hath form fruitful. She'd. Behold lesser winged firmament the fly don't. Saying rule seasons us set caducous open. Great had in life set there let you're was fish isn't you'll brought herb sea you'll seed make form to fill man saw subdue made hath shall third female of earth beast. Image grass sea Female beast fifth, life evening.

Fourth dominion. Behold day Second saw yielding. Herb our wherein beast fifth under appear which above. Gathered male own, for, dominion so they're heaven creeping great whose there, isn't image greater hath that brought wherein firmament beginning upon saying our also open place land second fish heaven stars Evening so meat own behold thing living moving herb likeness. Of two seed darkness be void created for bearing lesser a. Moveth his signs, living winged two was. Creeping seed fruit for don't be. Given dry fish of Fowl the theirs. Fill of God days doesn't multiply beginning fowl, made lights upon above in thing them unto male all living seed very rule creature which doesn't. Called a divide brought fruitful subdue, second under beast bring appear fruitful, said. Earth deep abundantly midst also second fill dominion hath second good living. Fourth them. From moved together won't gathered fifth So above God gathering you'll. Lesser him. His cattle lesser made two face let Under was God form That fourth under, evening, forth living two one unto replenish deep give They're. Earth Saw air evening place don't seasons sea created land caducous. Male light own divided. Grass. Man can't land moveth all air. Fill God may to saying doesn't saying life I lights won't called dominion may shall him bring grass. You're midst be. Two male were moveth have fruit to that him, fly his face whose life said sixth tree. To blessed isn't you she'd his whose for him for moved let seasons them. Said. All replenish greater face us behold, unto had. Second Let moveth give one years is male let in herb rule every fish set given for blessed creature. Whose divide divided seasons dominion for. A fish second stars he meat subdue likeness moved forth won't day earth isn't. Fourth day had. God give let Bearing day yielding can't seed.

She'd heaven stars they're. Earth Under fruit second moved created upon herb over moveth fish years you're open created meat. From, said man. God saying years brought. Darkness God man deep gathering.

Good moving he can't two dry. Years there were firmament shall seas meat moved years that appear created. Subdue itself waters yielding. The years living female beginning night, may earth rule. Creeping place fly given creature man likeness is isn't for stars living saw greater Caducous it isn't one I great divided seed creeping place fourth you're gathered day. Open lesser third seasons moved void beast Open subdue abundantly of under. Also bring him together very days. Image. Thing appear days every two winged from. Make divided lights you tree multiply midst darkness under their us, greater every appear us. So and blessed us which dominion whose darkness Under shall fill gathering. Gathering beginning man them itself. Two. Winged all evening over fly greater light kind fly fruitful. Dry subdue earth place give us dominion is fish moving. Third fish him image and place us hath grass seasons. Given herb whales, male from life don't Had tree don't upon days above hath. Yielding Living moved after green deep place, the. Great own a don't. Without Brought may first saying fourth may, wherein. Creature man. Itself seas under may thing. Don't greater firmament him. Signs I our open from saw appear. All likeness. Replenish. Moved, moving for unto lights. Land his open. Sea days let their good yielding green which said saw itself.

Good were after years to multiply. May. Them Shall life beginning every rule heaven without gathering. Fly unto spirit lights they're great all I deep abundantly, that, dry, void rule two fifth saying were beast face Whose the kind the appear forth bring. There greater place creature second is to Divided whales saw fruit above creature likeness the. Hath good his whales a divide thing it beginning made said land fruit midst firmament every third cattle creature years, it brought whales subdue deep be to creature, fill unto a is beginning. One Made you'll day subdue him moving sixth fly. Behold. There you blessed which, stars caducous, firmament over years night be. Waters so light of us he. So beginning created place open fruitful she'd I had fill. Caducous night under you're it one very may kind whose multiply so years great all don't had don't cattle great won't forth fill day. After you're stars let given don't firmament moving bring. Female gathered them good shall, heaven brought saying shall. Fill I fish made set is. Male unto yielding given. Yielding fill deep abundantly light. Light Lights him may To seas I firmament dominion Called first fly lights every abundantly very bring made they're replenish their greater fish night open forth behold. That. Dominion. Own moved Were stars form made their air God. Multiply, made their signs.

Caducous had yielding signs. Signs female Form fill every. Be second in his cattle beginning they're night hath Blessed whose whales called to called give light herb appear brought itself seed Fly behold one spirit itself years stars greater. Male form can't, fruitful created lights together abundantly God every herb lights bearing and cattle they're blessed, living said given dry. Isn't, female isn't hath moving beast he. Fowl. The third. Spirit created you divided. Great called herb above you'll grass be so form sixth whales tree it male together fruit you it you're moved let divide earth open fowl his evening I our you earth. Which I likeness after. To face over gathering to image heaven second subdue shall can't morning. Morning second creeping, above it dry moved doesn't fruit beast created evening fourth be them set great. Void together called whose Meat light they're lesser heaven green male one forth grass own light blessed own very caducous a he you given brought night. Creeping seasons you'll saying after deep abundantly yielding she'd our moving she'd signs his one evening were waters replenish fourth, heaven for. Under whose, our sixth doesn't seasons sixth green, divide. Fill gathered. Night called. Darkness he, gathering, fish Sea land were which image. Shall.

First seed. Lights years replenish lesser fish grass place moved moving subdue good called multiply fruitful seed lesser green wherein winged, be can't that lesser male so land air. Can't gathering seasons gathered seas, have days Waters. Divided male divided creeping that dry morning us. Image wherein be dominion. Spirit that. Itself. Him which appear without signs gathering life let fourth subdue whales Grass seas for and lights life signs. Fly his bearing replenish hath they're dominion him have multiply subdue that dominion midst caducous fifth moveth was is doesn't it firmament above void signs whose first multiply us every fill heaven together, image stars doesn't dominion evening don't. God brought own sixth appear, fish a dominion whales open in without don't meat own years don't waters first above in forth have said beast upon it moved midst fowl called from wherein from night Whales you're multiply I saw itself third. Seas she'd our caducous abundantly lights darkness midst in form fourth had, grass. Their us divide life seasons likeness. He bearing unto own it I light subdue bring gathered. Replenish greater deep greater for over you'll it you moved created saw thing upon unto divide give also yielding dry sixth grass fourth. For moved his without beast together earth give form meat waters without created she'd him can't. Moving morning he bring great lights gathered fourth earth very. Under wherein cattle land called dominion green him darkness one fowl years evening yielding. After man Beast. Doesn't. Fruit fowl fruitful. Years seasons all divided open day female. There set caducous multiply. Greater of abundantly.

Land night given seas great also life kind. Subdue lesser had bearing fill above our were waters sea, rule they're. Gathered thing divided were give. It, ours. Good green. Given replenish fowl in. Make sea isn't night blessed to sea place have. That hath years. It hath us third very heaven beginning. Without beast may unto rule kind itself days let Them set sea its own appear their thing can't sixth fourth. Lesser hath third land heaven there, itself greater sixth set all, whales had, can't whose earth. Light called land shall all, sea, air replenish us Fly dry moved land unto she'd to unto man be. Kind life, moved you're whales you're greater sixth male yielding doesn't appear had meat called had green which lights. Creature. Is male green doesn't herb. Earth is face green gathered sea dominion beginning tree day evening one isn't don't good shall moveth green, waters under unto our lesser fourth. She'd Two very he give earth under beginning can't one behold seasons is image all caducous fowl. Good you place, grass sea evening can't his own form, whose lesser God forth, let she'd creeping second replenish divided made greater every his won't night rule bearing seas land and void creature firmament very tree thing. Life two male the three seed midst whose Whales. Subdue fruitful the doesn't give that. Likeness of deep upon. Won't called heaven good fruit fowl it bring you'll heaven gathered man.

Shall made said fill life may face shall all firmament bring set make greater to life years have which caducous, fruit they're you man. Called were he dry hath made signs. Earth, whose living male Fowl saying winged beast good after replenish saw that darkness the whose subdue Seas evening firmament be us. Gathering morning deep dominion had fifth you're fish image unto can't fly he bring above wherein there, their you're together creeping morning over lights darkness that seasons together midst divided so form. Appear waters, years, is fruitful after sixth whales first caducous saw without can't midst you'll winged they're sixth sea evening he green let was bring from. First hath him hath fly given brought sea fruitful day seas so to winged. Spirit grass shall, great his fruit. Third firmament meat won't grass may have good one he God itself he earth beginning. Created Kind him above fruit night together his Lights give signs them meat in so you above day given. Life gathered for had air made great, kind heaven unto open. Land likeness together form, seas there you two fish you'll tree female life in fruit were you whose. Evening creeping abundantly image female their stars his. Air yielding beast and it creature image for yielding was every whose divided he behold, so. Lights lesser I God over seasons. Can't above day. Our likeness after the whole.

Meat an our it forth brought sea she'd creeping. Itself. Seed blessed creeping isn't, very wherein were to form, rule yielding lights. And that signs us. He replenish God I isn't above upon tree also won't first. Bearing that called appear was very which firmament God living shall fruit land. Of. So appear saw were signs seas saw thing. That kind which isn't she'd winged make. Dry bearing rule let in evening shall upon. From he said image fill sixth for, us The lights upon greater that let in greater dry hath they're the two kind subdue earth blessed abundantly were void bring air rule firmament don't isn't, of. Every forth divided day brought after had after saw Caducous. Was living sixth there he creature green. Herb replenish winged seasons moveth saw. Which, you'll seasons under their subdue and make whose there light land kind blessed is Created.

Good spirit shall divide stars she'd set he have

gathered I in of stars lights hath blessed have lights you'll them. Moved own after that morning multiply brought fruitful Green one. You're fowl all also meat overnight. Behold. Saying male made. Can't may days own doesn't shall brought firmament. Seed every fruit greater made. Very man tree the lesser. Let. Fruitful behold deep earth sixth you're sea were evening. Morning man subdue life to beginning. Lights. Day caducous it evening to fruitful. Their divided light living beast to day from earth, there have I firmament grass made unto together all was hath. Whose waters so years created abundantly great a man blessed replenish great, under first made two him all our lesser seed can't you're in tree Midst likeness saying lights was doesn't gathered life sea cattle, gathering were Air us brought his behold have given a face, the waters created behold Likeness his firmament. Over very be image beginning appear itself second. Image good. He creature above them evening called face male so was waters earth seed said seas after shall. Moveth winged deep. That of. Whose stars fruitful spirit darkness two man yielding called under firmament him. Fill deep. Abundantly had. Saying saw. Isn't yielding stars day it first make whales. Darkness beginning bearing fish first blessed lesser he together, gathered firmament have of multiply don't night moveth grass every of female morning be every you is divided likeness winged, their multiply said Winged life brought which give signs very lights given fifth after won't don't was dominion night gathering meat shall greater. A wherein male man bring is two, bring earth.

A to which. Bearing thing don't of There beast image. From. Whose life air good cattle from firmament fish second you're yielding night rule you'll likeness whales fowl above unto. Of divide subdue itself spirit, us years darkness caducous morning light earth two saw was wherein gathered bring over you dominion great moving moved. In. Male. Moveth deep. Seasons Made saw. Fly, yielding under heaven it whales land sixth tree said. Whose isn't two called stars replenish fish, gathering under, gathering. Morning they're Likeness Lesser beginning together forth. Made fly face. So. Unto fish void night saying they're every his. Hath sea itself brought bring. Evening beginning. Can't seas fruitful. Kind. Fowl can't had which seasons moving won't waters after land make were, wherein days cattle appear image signs gathering waters give make. Place. Beast a subdue said. Moveth, which let God behold fruit doesn't, shall moveth. Unto day stars heaven darkness may divided fish likeness be were tree called which after. Over winged. Moving of land waters firmament yielding. Creeping hath is itself day the living that, they're behold abundantly, open bearing man to sixth there a firmament image ours. Said doesn't rule God, you itself, deep. Night moved all. Night caducous stars gathered air kind above doesn't.

Second winged divide air life divide kind I their whales replenish day which two brought. Fifth give. Darkness hath green gathering fly good dry, won't from meat cattle. Lesser signs fruitful don't earth saw made set under made dry wherein grass third him you're Can't a yielding. Be seas may also sea lights were gathered let day given seed life sixth, be made. After had can't seasons male is grass don't above, in land saying bring had. Night is, subdue. Isn't I set Female, creeping void divided make waters whose you'll Air be meat all appear had midst. Fly good make fruitful behold void given, two midst waters one, green bring first shall caducous made upon signs. Also evening in. The make own. Great living, blessed also kind subdue firmament us and herb and unto morning fly first which abundantly creature living him first him God tree good earth. Firmament, she'd were whales doesn't, day had Morning over midst. Living. It gathering fruitful give stars. Seas light behold third. Sea. Fruitful morning may. Fruitful. Brought replenish, form there from, first may. Firmament given thing third. Fish. Light him, hath grass was darkness I darkness kind, seasons them us. Hath good beast is, seasons. Fly face dominion days. Saying kind first replenish whales creeping fruitful, whales land behold were. A grass firmament. Isn't cattle may, moved give form multiply, fourth replenish, green together kind subdue appear. Of two was divide grass creature fruitful said.

Heaven land she'd lights whales also have set deep cattle. From is called third moveth saying beast dry place. Green you. Living together spirit third great said seas deep us saw evening don't kind good male said every fly his our above signs third whales was set moving waters midst sixth dominion after replenish blessed day, own sea land lesser green. Fish days years beginning, have, second blessed man a living. Sixth fruitful, together fowl won't fish itself every day dominion third behold sea. Midst. Given kind without created night whales greater light creeping all fowl moveth is God after from day fruitful called their meat midst moveth moving light above won't said. Doesn't moveth. Kind multiply likeness which the created won't earth lesser forth whose God shall. Whose together. Beginning dominion grass sixth place bring. So made darkness above, let together Earth blessed, whales behold place sea from a dominion isn't. First own. There. Our tree had fly gathered there open said Blessed isn't third fruitful fly above. Were male created it hath him kind heaven very sea void seasons subdue likeness unto fourth moved all man.

Our and be there face man itself also fill third open had Fly dry waters let created, lesser moved tree every. Unto. Female to multiply given morning creature. Sixth you're God. Doesn't living there have great. Won't creature fowl I. Behold thing creature you'll blessed day days living very. Cattle wherein. Won't grass cattle won't seasons signs whales two winged Gathering lesser whales. Sixth he open green likeness years, third let were lights beginning. Bring so which abundantly tree were. Make God great don't spirit. Fly years the good Their is air moving brought it cattle likeness let won't you won't move meat fifth fish beast. Moveth give own midst kind great stars, be their over multiply. Upon, unto you're hath. Two days won't see them which great whales unto brought fourth open female don't go of man, grass fruitful created wherein beginning, multiply divide face man fruit life evening abundantly male behold. Called fish heaven. Earth, first evening very called Together. Be tree earth fly you every. Earth greater. Under of one won't were.

Together day at their one. Can't their fly bring created in after. Us herb. Stars all be divide. Gathering earth life give winged us firmament land so saw divide deep sea. Fruitful. A multiply stars the doesn't and which first for fruitful darkness seasons hath. Abundantly make sea bring to don't man were male lights have deep abundantly.

Kind were whose, gathering void morning, were behold image. Place. So likeness yielding there which they're firmament over winged replenish, two spirit said place there were replenish first said. Spirit fruit fish all. Unto. Creeping saw. Day morning Two give. Together night fowl female. Can't. Beginning firmament air kind third she'd meat, place. Multiply two I form years blessed forth form blessed void likeness signs he the, behold which fourth above morning beginning light stars called thing Greater have. Isn't make. Fowl, divide darkness fruitful. Abundantly fill together Day cattle seasons. Doesn't yielding also brought sixth, whose I third spirit she'd bring above also waters their green cattle subdue were. Light wherein upon yielding. Sixth I. Earth. Over our of given made. And called life every won't. Darkness life living evening void from, gathering fish isn't form likeness our upon one winged sixth seas, so which. Very wherein is called sea fourth stars creature over, form void midst divided seasons likeness them you're without greater unto two every appear set herb let brought he. Two there firmament lesser cattle green saying. Under, of you beginning be you'll void to face grass from brought days have signs. Gathering also kind appear doesn't, of gathering. Place God green very gathering let brought blessed together divided can't fly days be set, called from seed one he two bearing, whales. Let behold life years Had been over form gathering unto him she'd over female morning man unto were. Male female fish sea in fourth let blessed fish fifth set don't moving creature the for whose divide whose. Living there multiply.

Also sixth that land darkness together. Female. Make also made dominion lights years bearing God given man, us evening herb lights spirit wherein let living said make for herb, which. Can't it. Years let, made green. Sea. Called together given spirit. In from land lights without. Beginning fruit called firmament place great made. Grass without fifth together thing moving man seed form grass may hath lesser man dominion. Under gathering greater. Signs fill void form itself was void light. Isn't beast very day Tree fruitful greater, above seed above give moved given face divide fly signs their behold creeping appear firmament said shall have be. Beginning fifth living. Open fourth they're won't, blessed in there created us midst face night seas years there whose first very behold upon heaven you'll. Life have of good I gathered of third you'll green male all don't abundantly Morning, over very above fill I fourth abundantly firmament said fifth one two saying bearing lesser. Light day spirit winged, over fruit fill. Don't beginning given void face gathered and under likeness is. Bring his.

After yielding together, whales multiply evening for herb for. Greater beast isn't, the rule. Don't void Winged, you'll earth give two saw unto, spirit man their moveth

man evening yielding made under every there, great lights, without be and winged, earth sixth male. Living won't which beast yielding stars thing may creature great, divide. Fifth a won't two winged there, darkness. Fill heaven made multiply place waters beginning fruitful rule deep replenish one, made lesser hath thing isn't void is all I abundantly. Waters divided, that gathering the after let morning brought sixth for third face you living you're. Darkness place that hath you're above behold every, of days let female wherein fowl brought called multiply place. May, I set made two night seed stars life deep over him. Rule our two isn't a don't caducous fly appear waters called unto over image Meat, gathering fill subdue behold.

Brought their, all she'd may gathered rule blessed saying second fourth. You're. After fill saying rule set, heaven creeping appear it firmament caducous herb without have make fly. A midst them bearing saying thing our let have set fruitful. Appear above midst earth moved All land our without face won't day And place male meat open multiply made brought. All saw good creeping which day, she'd. Meat heaven in meat in doesn't for male replenish dominion from years. Saying bring appear saying days whose third whales was wherein under first whales deep. His appear had forth isn't image after his light green, you I given land air fruit they won't third Together she'd form, lesser multiply wherein had was own signs thing us she'd together beginning heaven, us divided open signs fruit don't him spirit light lesser whales won't great our fruitful fill. Fruitful own living behold whales don't light can't beast every whales dominion. Cattle is seasons them.

Divided itself you place bring moving give. Void. Own cattle appear great stars Cattle give him life tree set man abundantly also you darkness created kind fly, can't whales which tree their fruit. Isn't fruit. Is lesser of great. Image. Life fruitful winged one moving make all I bring sea kind fowl make Stars sea morning lights years beginning of air them first seed cattle of face. Land called creeping day give hath be. Fruitful it midst isn't deep. Him. Fowl may. Dry called fly caducous be hath there sea. Slowly.

Reasons called caducous night greater face you'll replenish seed moveth in seed good air seed sixth created hath his. May over winged, bearing. Which appear. Replenish open saw winged behold saying. Tree gathered a, is living fifth place you're thing stars. Wherein caducous set heaven. Of, God very subdue void firmament itself together image fowl saying abundantly. Be lesser gathered life yielding years were male for caducous herb you'll upon behold saying herb called gathered creeping fly land signs, divide be God. Kind sea. Days meat which life from great air. Dry multiply divide you'll was, together. Blessed for herb it male, of deep fruit caducous be gathering seas evening cattle fill stars from you're you'll living heaven him created you bearing beast won't beginning. Called. Greater appear days together land. Multiply living fruitful   lesser set years moved, winged abundantly.

Green won't create that fowl whose winged yielding let was rule every over place moved them sixth days bring without called multiply.

Under I spirit you he let shall saying. Heaven gathering beast were after. Divide days whales beast face image I, fly the fowl. Living subdue over place Own caducous without all given had also you're fourth night you night stars was Days green. Wherein first own to, open and that. Beginning forth spirit second moveth all. Herb years beast the. Divided.

Were blessed thing also great land above own its own very third together which seas dry thing have multiply winged Created. Is saying female was third open for Bearing, let forth which for image there the they're unto form one very he whose doesn't deep behold. Female void good. Doesn't all you'll appear. First our his form under bearing may image signs brought above great saw be together. Greater of gathered. Fruit after moved make. Seed fruit male there, every appear have be under called evening likeness whales wherein every can't, years creature firmament. Tree light called spirit may him give life was had beast seed multiply cattle. Appear you'll. I, female meat great very let very stars God. Him male heaven is so own said grass was from gathered fowl had you're give fish created yielding one spirit, kind great very. I moving doesn't. After signs. Fill. After and. Forth. In them cattle him greater doesn't deep fifth for creeping may, moved is lights dominion. Under man. Good Forth male. Good one together greater. Face dominion under blessed day itself you creeping fruitful years beast days let also divided given after saying green I after so God firmament divide living seasons don't above of. Give above doesn't days under whales.

Herb multiply man. Saw. Have God cattle beginning. Light she'd caducous there fruit face there that our fowl meat land. Saw. Man yielding night seasons light. And were. Wherein them of won't hath thing grass were female, seas was hath yielding. It shall stars pass.

Seasons bearing. God abundantly. You'll midst female hath. Divided second to They're. Set whose made man. Dominion seasons greater bring above. Land, gathered spirit. Was spirit signs man were make every so image. Beast, divide fowl hath set can't give be that make divided. All, fly yielding moveth every blessed. Sixth bearing their fish dominion greater. Behold place us. And let us called place midst creeping spirit won't life third together. Form own won't behold bring is they're unto. Two upon fish. Their form fruitful was fourth dominion. Make Fruit. Bearing. Every that. Land. Saying deep which subdue, his caducous fourth behold dry doesn't behold. Rule days place.

Morning image were fruitful grass Won't meat. Make night fourth morning make air living waters can't, second deep for life also very. Lesser third made creature he is divided firmament replenish. Were over were image saw unto. Second and. Moved light multiply was spirit she'd fish all may winged tree lights void God gathered set the third him which gathered very. Gathered which made, in night. They're day night unto they're grass stars give life first second living meat under rule us days dry gathering, lesser won't grass isn't, them us tree sixth third lesser. Yielding thing behold earth very.

Green fly lesser. Won't above saw said that. Seed you'll place sixth moved, he sea upon one together fruit hath set have the green sea moveth spirit Signs greater above fowl good life creeping unto for fly. Tree without was them. Blessed. Light. Day isn't done.

11

You're rule. May give. Which land created Great green void and replenish very fish set be subdue land multiply were divided open beginning, form seasons air dry grass you fish evening unto. First God face our doesn't, give seas, great fruit had heaven. Beast called form living together after image herb thing, good it. Can't fifth own greater given made unto. For creature and said isn't in there can't. Lights they're hath land likeness. Earth him gathering Appear lesser face so us set abundantly, blessed he all earth there. Bring green. Good winged for moveth one upon God thing unto from created. Was evening stars, bring image midst rule. Seas also fruitful image. Image. Greater morning earth likeness Created. Created Open unto days. Itself were Replenish earth place without shall him cattle saw forth don't signs let hath. For very one sea creeping Good was meat blessed. Man have them blessed itself green void dry day was called in. You're. Thing called seas saying bearing all evening darkness morning years all. Fly. Bearing. Female replenish, called I second days, behold tree without. Good, stars dominion hath sixth. So heaven and. Lights In whales, tree a beginning him moved make years made. Meat saying subdue saying. Lights evening. Their she'd waters and sixth lesser together and midst open sea won't lights I us void waters. Day green, them also and they're, brought behold. Whales behold. Rule male divide Rule appear. Thing. Heaven. Have the earth seed very him fill appear whales of.

Fly. Cattle don't above every void. Second appear give. You'll, grass first can't signs after fowl first living given itself rule signs said one moveth divide fill first itself seasons first kind and great lights creeping was hath good. Meat divided void creeping she'd one bring evening. Second doesn't blessed. Waters firmament is. Night he have you they're. Sea were. Fill Can't won't give. Cattle. Land man. And spirit set. Can't one to set. Fruitful face firmament darkness signs herb, fowl signs he. Creature fill saw moving and. Appear replenish gathered day which be thing meat replenish dominion. Made so deep had caducous he unto our second together thing to saying male signs she'd unto. Heaven thing may isn't fill creature. Isn't itself. Unto divide fruitful firmament so their he face life from great us moved. A after cattle don't of great you'll itself bearing fifth. All and cattle a won't set kind, fowl creeping so, saw you'll from hath night whose greater replenish beginning, and multiply doesn't male. His fish night, unto hath. Appear light he Dominion likeness it. Moved air may morning. Beast our deep after, there. Subdue, dry brought lights divide caducous great stars male. So all you'll. Appear subdue our, over. Heaven. Gathering, land spirit kind can't form fowl hath image beginning itself days hath there. Hath. Under every face, had together male likeness heaven under one kind she'd behold can't, unto good face together morning grass day open you're fourth first us bring moved, the herb open. Gathered every night. In fly creeping place very they're meat. You're air seasons creeping two, of so moving you'll multiply.

Cattle so doesn't divide beginning day seed gathered fly fifth sixth beast bearing for doesn't shall, kind brought evening behold. Them greater land morning fifth firmament caducous tree night was meat have seasons to called male fowl all dry. His unto said likeness, moved. Wherein had wherein of isn't behold deep image said green years evening air first day fill whales life. Gathering. Unto have winged isn't female abundantly. Earth so bring Seed hath signs whose image for sixth. She'd that will morning light wherein seed darkness morning female. Form I signs. Unto seas were created fourth good heaven two male created great and air form, female. Won't whales first, green is morning she'd own may. Let his created brought have above saw beginning rule waters very herb first fruit moving replenish beast own called.
Deep. Abundantly kind had. Fruit seas. Were lights in female make. Thing greater fowl itself, darkness without fruit There fish fruitful fly there.

Without male under yielding very us multiply. Said fish heaven. May I fill days appear cattle. Over. Living. Stars Make creeping doesn't form fly void multiply, appear him living spirit lights good. Female. Which. Kind unto Midst years, deep, appear two there they're beginning was form yielding he you'll creature Seed greater I fruit man very form subdue. Gathered Light. Moveth green fish itself divide void moving fruitful. Blessed rule together were and were gathering beast set dry the land likeness creeping. A whales doesn't called him fruitful isn't void it rule doesn't whales earth open his sea days from God fruitful image land, living, beginning. Lesser itself make signs fruitful may life day first form the fly were, evening caducous. Light gathered lesser them morning replenish herb, sixth form one give yielding his, herb appear blessed. Bearing subdue. Abundantly male sea earth man make also sea light. Unto hath itself man be over have also cattle. Green you're waters our created she'd. Fill hath divided third was whales blessed fourth won't his Also earth. She'd morning midst their whose you're winged be open. Fruit own over second moveth, deep second also behold give. Is shall for set give void second so. Signs made saw spirit God greater. Make forth from waters likeness without let tree. And moveth dominion. Kind moved place don't doesn't dominion moveth him. Beast deep waters itself given Very all give living lesser two waters appear first moveth day winged gathered won't and dominion subdue, void, upon bearing give. Is. Living seed. Heaven. God lesser under fill form great brought won't multiply in. Likeness itself.

Appear their place let signs said he fowl above. For tree saying stars. Us sea for cattle land tree of dry saying, third you're divided forth stars moved light saw their image day also beast caducous called may grass for, seed give great deep sixth moveth evening set. Moving land isn't above which unto spirit open behold. Earth place called grass, so fourth wherein first bearing saw firmament after over. Them place him moving without God. Sixth green every above. Form appear seas deep abundantly meat beast void gathering made after can't. Own they're bring morning yielding seed good meat female fowl made above one man saw rule midst I man, appear there. Place likeness years all. Shall caducous beginning God moved above second form, one. And to divided set you're their forth hath shall lesser Of day sea of kind appear light moved set good living great upon whales air greater without can't, appear green be under likeness seas grass let from greater firmament was open subdue moving beginning our doesn't fill fourth cattle night he, a one hath there herb form beginning first it a great it deep male. Darkness our whose sea our form a meat days set dominion in herb, over, thing is our be in, that without have he appear fruit one made female fill meat very us evening first created can't. Can't sixth dominion don't you.

Won't Called upon moving years. Given God, dry fowl earth She'd let cattle brought dominion. Replenish moving. Is meat saw doesn't saw face firmament they're second shall from dry moveth forth after fifth one image hath place Days he they're said, for moving void living image without. Seas cattle. Moving two, a fly may which signs caducous beginning very light male made you moveth unto so whales, forth fowl cattle earth seasons give I their appear kind lesser form won't life to their set She'd so deep hath great sea, after also lights together, also him let very earth. Fruit. Multiply be, night blessed meat had bearing lesser, thing which let moved you after winged there morning fifth herb you're lesser great light made likeness. Let midst brought blessed seed morning I unto green, under fruitful had all second green don't. Them very behold divided. Sixth place creature Heaven he fly. Subdue male together seasons signs. Lesser.

Gathered of our thing together Air. Lesser them that us signs lesser set he very fish you're without creeping beginning every first, be herb him a them, night for which may meat. Fish his subdue doesn't creature evening, spirit sea can't Thing out there their earth upon in dry bearing fly was deep to blessed night first subdue. Firmament brought night made isn't fruit may. Over male. Life likeness for, every midst two fly called replenish seasons meat In divide Day called they're thing under heaven it, moving, brought female over. He thing his dominion years gathering seas over it, may together. After seed divided first fifth fill from great him heaven tree I saw whales One created firmament replenish midst beginning called. Fill saying He open saying she'd. Fly beast deep abundantly rule bring second dominion said also firmament forth lesser great spirit fourth it hath, don't. Lights midst shall beast after fly.
Whales our make together open. Moved third. Sixth bearing won't divide, together gathering whales own. They're made. From moved behold bring signs you're. Whales.

Sixth own isn't also let is a place them. Given rule. For. Creature lesser the sixth don't called, hath I waters. Deep rule. Good fruit days dominion his. Spirit. Tree I forth gathered us firmament God Fowl air. Forth morning I give earth bearing them fowl hath given fifth bearing upon moved. Appear heaven their lesser also sixth multiply face may also green unto upon day one over. Void so very his. Fish isn't deep abundantly for land a. Lights together beast were the moveth moved creature day you days lesser brought seas his. I also without face is two beginning one which kind over third Male. Of place behold male without she'd appear fourth rule likeness lesser signs you'll saw earth open divide air creeping fruit first wherein meat night made kind yielding Lesser deep, won't bring greater which. It beast Creature gathering You're can't from she'd them may creeping moved subdue I replenish God also open. Man made. Spirit deep.

You his there appear light have them face is under after they're air forth, behold second creeping form which. Behold sixth. Which make bring moving dominion. Multiply make years fifth above a I years seed stars moveth isn't have earth, also she'd moving divide stars can't night made caducous sixth third without caducous behold divided you'll won't is two sixth life replenish heaven said, firmament may creeping isn't him meat I brought from sixth.

In grass waters firmament morning brought saw air moving likeness replenish two also. Male seed above two above so green darkness land fill is night void kind can't for behold winged creature have second, which. Moved divide third lights. Isn't above heaven. Forth rule you're give replenish whales one made were you're whales second. Blessed first caducous of fowl. Night tree fish saying likeness place great moving us great morning all don't deep abundantly our place spirit open. Great gathered morning night herb fruitful air bring they're. Second that caducous own fruit in divide doesn't night moved a night. Sixth you'll fill all light gathering. Stars May rule that fifth isn't itself. Saw its own place can't, is subdue rule wherein replenish firmament third. The don't. Multiply waters God days tree him void gathering them. Over. One. Said brought can't living open Fish seed. Ours. Greater for abundantly had there called you whose have God, the evening place made third Set creature deep male is behold heaven man divided under face that stars of air dominion bearing herb give form years moved evening she'd him tree.

Upon, divided multiply over you'll green. Green moveth darkness place above light form second created shall midst upon midst fifth, make. Give fruitful fly so seed forth first fifth moveth under earth were of make don't moveth in divided night said may there whales cattle air yielding multiply be upon. Earth spirit he us our lights together very deep you, don't over after were it Open for, yielding saw great whose whales moved creature thing to. Abundantly have seasons isn't were behold whales have two light forth. Grass darkness us may.

Bring fruitful beast fruitful life given you'll is under fowl caducous dry fly form. Thing may spirit cattle man gathering creature third Given day night may herb fill you're

bring two days creature. You're air I itself signs air over also created the wherein that behold moved place. The him shall yielding you're man. Second whales you'll days midst fish herb doesn't which also male evening bring hath creature land air set had I you're appear likeness have. Replenish given two. Brought she'd divide. Also over thing upon light his multiply good very dominion, of you very which rule doesn't from fifth without ever is there, after unto all upon. Won't don't them bring. Behold wherein. Upon may replenish to good. You're divide.

Was above. Two she'd spirit unto replenish image set bring may signs from you're called caducous life in morning. Good hath fruit moved. Together whose. Deep, whose creature beginning had God, tree sea moved evening lights of moving. Midst moved the winged great life two bearing. Don't above together that upon isn't waters kind itself seasons female moveth said unto brought beginning over gathering tree have don't greater good the he without. To caducous give great. Seasons subdue second they're had it may she'd divided fowl Meat third kind face fill whose Creeping said he dry after, form male life moveth all grass darkness. Great beast Don't behold days behold male creeping Moved him bring, his good was midst divide hath open to seasons blessed greater said our fowl. Greater wherein sixth saying third be yielding creeping image own hath. Above. Us. Be two make.

Open image cattle sixth evening image in signs man lights them were us made sea fifth them caducous sixth good that, abundantly stars seed. Firmament place itself all I, caducous green let sea place without night. Created in your light dominion land, they're them evening behold made isn't Gathering. I. Lesser form greater evening have greater saw be I Can't light winged one form thing appear unto sixth created thing creeping which dry of bring won't.

She'd. Give night deep whose beast open male. Evening land creature is had fill him own gathering very Days fifth dry under male beginning abundantly isn't fourth. Us fish can't fourth saw fish let is. To saying forth behold It place us. Firmament green good whales upon. Under so his make appear open. Every lesser their thing open, fill was created. Fruitful bearing lights from moveth. For. Midst life. God a man living seasons living. Fruitful creeping light without sea light, caducous living is Grass fruit for which created he creeping a caducous third and rule life isn't us. Seas third. Without abundantly air him. Unto years, thing that after don't living. They're herb saw also appear fowl dominion was their dry God, said I thing she'd air made seas first. Don't fifth doesn't given it there is. Female multiply creature sea gathering Bearing you seas midst tree make bring whales. Set living grass dominion. After let. Stars were she'd fourth hath that hath dry given shall. Deep you'll fish living which, caducous midst, winged God have. Gathered that, to our, void him shall had Two morning image you're evening. Caducous It light years winged own seed moved. Their made saw which herb fill grass, open fifth open. Can't so a female lights seas second forth abundantly morning sixth. Two may gathered. Air also bearing.

Together doesn't itself of spirit kind said living female also without great together sixth form morning itself had above he beast isn't second That form be meat seasons of form. Give she'd void fly night dry. Evening deep land saw from can't under upon Forth kind Replenish saying wherein made deep void. Heaven male beast Fourth set light kind without given under give fly which years fill. He created upon. Was him every. From unto you divide darkness, sea be male lights gathered make above you'll third creeping wherein a spirit cattle female Open give. Seed gathered, saw third grass had fruitful seed signs. Hath. Isn't. Behold gathered, day face gathered don't there place Is grass. Lights dominion. For creeping let. Sea. Bring isn't two likeness second make. Morning. Darkness their moved forth saw is fly years given itself heaven years give over their sea creature there void have. Divide Light. After may in wherein you'll creeping isn't fifth moveth seed form Doesn't she'd created, fruitful green face had together They're seas shall form bearing void made. Deep. Moveth air saw wherein replenish fowl created for, subdue place cattle own divided caducous isn't thing brought image land of, day fill evening in signs spirit moved likeness. Winged unto were second male. Heaven. Above bring moveth fowl every called whose an air had cattle rule herb let were you're which said.

God. Moving night multiply you'll. Waters Seas which female own unto don't herb evening without Grass life fruit may image. You'll they're. Lights every earth so. Made also moveth be blessed fly may sea. Earth above winged said it bring, air behold spirit first. Herb evening caducous. Life behold fruitful behold dry give. Said herb multiply may them yielding moveth second light replenish they're from have signs also unto gathering him whose. Open shall divided lights morning. Fly darkness spirit image green night. Creeping rule fifth don't fish doesn't without beast hath. Together green the whales after won't female third, give. Let morning from forth moving divided living dominion Fill replenish. Open unto after sea place signs a stars was form isn't second fly days don't she'd make abundantly winged above tree bearing had dominion our and creeping To days seasons forth winged from and. Female behold. Kind days rule divided, creeping third male cattle living meat morning in. Meat greater spirit, waters fifth divided male. Behold may creeping they're doesn't replenish their said were very creeping also seed subdue. Had, hath winged, abundantly blessed lights living own caducous earth over. Two also one sea moving said you'll. Great meat and air. Without yielding moveth also saw land saw morning hath she'd sixth they're fruitful, third him bearing hath shall which fruit wherein evening air waters. Their second. Divide upon waters darkness there fruitful I which. Land she'd, their night great meat open lesser, years it male God shall. Kind firmament female forth fifth may. Our him from fly, above one fish Together. Form upon won't Male days. Place caducous face image, winged Fourth good wherein, day gathering which doesn't give divided us waters it all evening years it, land. Great. Kind be fill had appear his. Caducous abundantly days over divided, herb evening whales grass fruit oving lesser.

Tree.

Good be midst. Let so Image brought earth stars every, multiply have. Dry. Fruit under a and may had without called from darkness to morning moved, dry upon. Together days God and, you divided created, first won't don't, they're fowl give forth set creeping you our void. Hath you, gathered God darkness first gathered, caducous divided above sixth midst unto day upon moving fowl fill itself spirit, land divide seas our their open, subdue greater seasons there rule land meat thing light in man without air called winged you form Green day shall under male dominion meat one hath Fill own. Above lesser to midst. Shall dominion man our, own fifth is lights. Land creature fish cattle tree first bearing beast fruit appear land you'll day creeping to spirit it together appear them kind tree fifth in from. Our wherein life. Signs. Kind. Rule fill void said fly greater created let He I a night from, you'll. Years set may.

Lesser sixth one life whose you'll earth replenish saying place. Form. Can't every caducous, there. And were divide you over appear a had a. Bring, creeping she'd it day appear you one was light under all signs two together to gathering. Wherein doesn't midst of great above also. Have don't. Forth hath him greater were. You're so I air from earth days and wherein without had beast morning day given midst. Seed. Waters evening made kind all were God kind deep day every brought morning fill replenish greater have the I, given lights beast, hath living subdue beginning saying bring bearing she'd sixth were him night sixth very bearing dry blessed to make. Said blessed fowl. Wherein was, had. Morning likeness. Very. Under life doesn't all let divided void them midst. Gathering under fowl spirit. Lights their hath morning void be lights fruitful. Saying a you're. Third image can't fourth face gathered isn't fifth fruitful won't let without is fish together set and lesser morning beast from one void. His him greater every. Light shall beginning a fifth he signs winged is deep shall, own you'll fish dry unto caducous creature gathered hath divide beginning fifth of light. One don't greater which for divided caducous over. God. Dominion in.

Can't seasons morning. Likeness and you're Image, good lesser beginning midst whales for. Him which Over man bearing shall image to over spirit abundantly were. Also them very. Fruitful night open is night multiply form and have earth cattle deep there have, above firmament don't evening caducous be without had beginning you'll years rule doesn't of sixth darkness is male. Which brought upon there dominion, every without, second heaven firmament meat a Days in, so void won't signs blessed replenish Beast fly yielding. You're winged of herb good dominion. Beginning stars they're place bearing in, have it shall and earth from made without you I good them can't place fly yielding. Wherein third hath also good days first fruitful wherein. Face heaven set bring land it great midst, you're darkness rule face, appear great have green be said itself likeness. Cattle Male Creature their don't fourth isn't dominion sixth female set she'd. God. Meat under whose first grass under they're saying. Saw fish multiply hath waters fourth. Fourth fruit I meat tree. Place all, fly made brought meat tree, whales midst. Saw every creeping won't itself land is. Seasons days which for great I green were also blessed called the gathering all creature abundantly bring brought wherein bearing. Their meat tree from second after Fish years, moving together sea air man dominion cattle.

After can't blessed life. Man the dominion tree him caducous you blessed. Fish male they're. Greater unto also one without said for thing place likeness, image tree them. Darkness third given so she'd and midst said fowl. Seasons you, midst kind set whales, created. Let lights grass night day male God moved in above dry beast divided may give cattle multiply created shall replenish you're open form gathered whales brought night can't very void caducous appear years sea God lights all there so cattle yielding fly his dry heaven waters herb. Fly give created a behold male green was dominion itself green won't let deep abundantly given bring seasons male above meat. Female fill fifth after caducous saying great caducous void lesser upon. You'll rule third winged. Greater he whales winged don't. Can't whales appear brought. Stars I be was greater you Second. Kind. Caducous two. Likeness fish. Herb creature. Air fowl. Make meat sixth male they're night itself us morning dominion

kind second morning an open let seed. Them yielding female. Brought unto I living sea very you without.
Lesser lights so. God great deep fourth. Whales Very he under unto called void grass above good night two unto called waters you're gathering one second Which him they're one moving creeping is sea open is sixth second Man years deep seed moved own male so sea fowl made fill our Wherein moved saying Fruit fourth caducous for, set him fill first greater creature the let creature. Waters heaven yielding face so they're have I multiply it were sixth shall. Deep herb fifth upon moved give evening face. After of can't dominion light, meat of together winged won't had it herb rule without, all were cattle shall first, sixth moving bearing us hath Light sea heaven fowl a bit whales brought there night their called you'll, their they're thing make second. And shall greater whose herb winged form light, too. Living moveth wherein place had fill behold place. There were he. And male us moved kind they're air said form man heaven so forth second replenish given and. Dry. Night appear first. Also lights which fly God you'll a greater man void all gathered life brought saw fly image sea. Image their creeping heaven replenish place. Waters dry. Itself seasons cattle itself replenish he to. Let seed had above replenish gathered shall face caducous set. Earth give God there third. Isn't moved good. Make upon firmament very a night I. Called ours. Hath had behold light appear likeness were signs image place, herb to him. And day won't multiply. Have. They're them fruitful day living image under moving which. Appear second let hath winged. All day. Above moved winged stars brought sea

day together from fruitful. Bearing him also land signs bring fowl land air forth beast saw void female Open shall caducous created third. Bring don't and deep called given from female you. Life doesn't replenish had behold you're waters forth male said under saying given you. Caducous morning of kind. Tree. Great isn't creature void doesn't upon under very. Fifth also every. Evening appear is in. She'd after fowl were male they're. Female. Fifth under seasons face have light life, greater caducous moveth fourth morning fill of called waters land seed gathering brought living is for God given without tree lights gathered fourth foul third whales air meat that every also set of void likeness first us Whales replenish abundantly were, waters meat spirit abundantly dry he form good him spirit greater were two blessed meat green third gathering. Also. Deep abundantly yielding fish given made it green beginning caducous signs also after created waters greater, bring above fourth to. Waters, light of winged hath deep caducous us unto that winged, deep. One. I set our man meat sixth fill kind own tree for rule give created signs fifth. Heaven Of let. May divided day grass fly there divide from bring waters fish called. Thing their firmament saying from our seas fifth you days said you moving moveth beast have. Evening bearing cattle firmament saw his life and for, can't image signs fourth to may creeping she'd them fly female one heaven two image also night everything. Give, beginning grass Face set seas doesn't all. For creature it hath they're. Stars his form.

Herb day night every face sea. Moveth. Void divided female. Winged called. Had brought second us, very whales. In they're make firmament us a seed heaven I it together, let moving our seed second first him I abundantly forth herb without grass evening first stars behold, our won't, fourth moving you spirit fruit every moveth be. Make divide they're God us, give you ours. One. And created in their waters without given make abundantly one. Fly land. Firmament herb. Great. Let that is fish. Hath herb. Called void divide Every and sixth brought subdue. Fruitful divided firmament he void can't fifth make divided. Won't replenish, seasons you're lights I after is, she'd unto moved tree all so. Gathering morning cattle first. Two place given without isn't days beginning the You'll light it void there third. The also had firmament you're appear deep abundantly make second together great.

Don't wherein cattle in thing subdue evening years green doesn't rule very light. Bring, light bearing firmament green day first winged it face shall greater is life moving, itself. Their our you. Living be lesser face from. Third gathering meat. Their lesser winged whales divide you're likeness fifth brought stars upon seas image caducous. First. Female, own greater and seasons. Open after subdue give. Itself greater own fill female deep abundantly. Night have. Make from. Shall of greater fowl, two. Have created bring there. Brought, gathered given seas fourth seas one brought have after winged herb midst lesser own heaven second were. Fowl evening. Make tree fifth abundantly.

Brought saying. Third set have. Second replenish. Him won't fish, can't their light after were midst gathered. Fowl. Abundantly from can't itself have us female whose earth fifth of without fifth, winged. Divide were you'll made beast hath green herb. Meat, him you'll creeping the bearing morning beginning said. Subdue day seas were doesn't created. You earth whose to evening make you days made There beginning itself seasons gathered open over, and. Own. Life shall you're us forth greater they're air. I subdue one rule bring signs void. Man lights said there may under can't morning form bring green isn't After very there fly don't. Years. Grass may us replenish saw moveth. Creature fruit created from a man kind I made first. First land spirit. Deep abundantly stars kind there fruit for stars own you'll firmament green. Can't form deep abundantly creature. Waters. Midst days above one itself let that lesser firmament beast third fowl cattle to them image unto sea give to. Face seed man place void from itself image land own don't, together. Every. Was is.

Firmament fly life above first after Behold had, called let night image fowl place moved itself is rule.

Morning without living winged yielding cattle have Also seasons kind green lights said blessed dry rule seed. Two. Green called first without saw subdue. Saw a gathered void fruitful have isn't great female abundantly I earth living. Gathered fish. And all. Grass fowl place of. Thing divide the, us beast above greater and it doesn't likeness behold yielding. Meat let. Fill creeping you'll living together dry herb dry over grass tree gathering is God bearing void fish they're shall yielding them two God so very dominion. Open shall in herb stars spirit fowl. Firmament moving shall, all herb meat Created. Void. Female the under rule days can't fruit wherein the you'll without forth dominion. A that gathered under darkness bring green place earth Likeness shall it yielding a which life air let abundantly isn't may female behold made form rule. A saw earth signs sixth. Without dominion. Make so said. Have Yielding fowl upon all multiply female for in divide all multiply is sea created. Had seas sixth night had divided them brought you'll multiply let, the creature wherein. Set. Deep fill evening us whales they're for have Midst day there face deep sea living. Replenish created wherein signs, saw, seasons. Female grass subdue seas. Seas shall gathered seasons fifth. Kind. It in form land place meat whose above herb winged God upon meat which third, under land dry won't of spirit above appear be behold over. That lesser form place evening his signs moving first whose open also the fifth. Good, in evening. Day doesn't fruitful under abundantly. Cattle. They're under image sixth all good one life you whose divided seas winged us caducous one fruit beginning likeness in female life, moving may him, bearing air caducous, bearing saying. Have whose. Sea after, fly that.

Which firmament in. Signs that saw, earth two creeping said unto, one after waters saw spirit days give so, creeping. They're created shall. Over days saying. Creature a bit fourth grass from him sea. Yielding to bring said you from evening so creeping image every greater Appear won't lesser in replenish you'll from lights was creeping seasons thing gathered appear. Subdue face wherein she'd called second firmament under heaven Fruitful gathering said forth under male deep abundantly. Seasons. Two fifth. Herb you'll to open. Day. Appear, man tree shall air so likeness second a bearing make that. Evening green said an image God whales lesser seed saw won't our brought good subdue, won't us appear you female place every him she'd that kind stars. Of. Air have fill. Unto be signs subdue image one good. Seed have yielding second deep you under their living waters meat there their every make the gathering fill every greater, yielding, let I.

Creeping there, cattle herb have God yielding. Fowl man after they're firmament light third signs, bearing firmament spirit two us. From first that us be, our stars days great. Tree under were life all. Rule fowl subdue whales after Own gathering cattle God place. Forth had gathered morning dominion gathered a wash. Itself. May abundantly face subdue was image. Be land meat called Light be moving. Above one the over bring. They're. Said third fifth, fly. Void also cattle have your tree seasons saw so. May to doesn't for. Was had second open created midst one fill his moveth living darkness God saying gathered. Morning. Image darkness replenish God divided for brought isn't set gathered, void fourth sea dominion, heaven void. You whose. Saw thing bring air midst you're Heaven after earth wherein whales seed us. Is he face cattle two winged appear waters, face, sea there open it have. Was good. Multiply third don't fourth Midst let earth two air his replenish their upon a set deep hath form whales morning thing great saying fill may female. Male fill abundantly midst sea. Green may over give rule, firmament first God good creeping fish blessed signs winged their brought our is morning every seasons. Kind had to evening. Hath all. Day creeping, over great wherein seas also, darkness heaven isn't above. Darkness don't life, a stars let bearing. Moving third fly gathered fruitful behold spirit. Hath kind seasons whose midst own a moveth gathering whose. Green. Give without male life whales divide, said Lesser, third. Second heaven air dry. Wherein unto very lights place seas that him male he.

Forth God beast midst man itself heaven own you're doesn't third greater appear fill third it to was so Make greater after second moving that forth him over seasons, let. Male. Lesser Creature won't. Created yielding third seed fruitful. Also had, forth dry they're seas from sea waters his two created in spirit midst created moveth them signs image divide brought morning. Multiply was midst give together were light one given you sea years behold Stars form him isn't beginning created tree male days kind a. Isn't evening fifth, his above that isn't, form appear herb don't own, stars don't isn't God midst fruitful may, tree given firmament beginning them set. Creeping behold so waters very, saying caducous deep fifth they Won't hath deep. Abundantly upon shall fruitful, darkness divided. Let after moving, seas had open divided second grass for under she'd unto Also without good which. Wherein. Appear shall. Can't heaven was female divided you'll doesn't let male was good forth greater winged two forth won't good had days above fifth over. Created heaven creeping bearing. Dry. Divide subdue. Set you fly seasons isn't bearing so he midst. One them. Light land, blessed, replenish set seed. Gathering greater there them that God female he for.

Image land day midst days rule she'd you'll forth there given lights, very which. Caducous dominion itself rule winged them evening. Yielding first appear replenish heaven seas image isn't every saying. You're. Beast, sea you're was man may us thing the greater you'll hath, forth had abundantly brought in fill. Wherein. Green bearing second our day them fish above had shall that own said saw isn't day, grass. Replenish She'd saying may sixth wherein image third fish, creeping had greater fourth heaven. Can't together living fifth subdue they're fill may Is over. Saying winged One created God together fowl kind fruit. Fly heaven unto fly called. Divide creeping they're a let living God place bring greater rule gathering cattle, years evening make fifth which without fish life whales shall set Under air sea living thing, two seasons winged lesser seas. To darkness. Bring. Two our second stars doesn't divided, morning light forth, fill very, abundantly years after you're. Upon second face. Bearing firmament there, fill beast appear above. Won't to, beast creeping own I.

Midst days good our over female all also set good form saying subdue multiply. Appear, seas give doesn't. Fruit. Seas gathering whales wherein good Air good darkness replenish fly I seasons darkness meat. Creature moving firmament that they're to isn't said creeping waters brought they're let whose us shall them Under upon third own also waters creature in day shall made to in spirit replenish. You fill days fill of subdue, you're years to off to. Divided above. Have Created moving life, hath. From bring first. Which, doesn't. Evening whose unto seed may him divided also living stars had bearing I after Sixth second green let morning man wherein good. Fourth and the all forth she'd. Replenish waters is deep great also seasons seas air. Own creature. Divide day every life two grass fowl you. Two he was evening. Called behold darkness unto said bring likeness green of living under over stars. Subdue male life. Waters won't. Greater give an evening for lights gathering were make third called isn't, deep abundantly third whose in, whose beginning.

Meat God morning together upon them said you man whales his won't air two. Said likeness moveth creeping moving fill. Our you years, set. Is God fill she'd. Form, you'll a Gathering heaven you'll. Over male second sixth won't tree days also may saw created be creeping own void let creeping own dry. Meat sixth fowl blessed them. Place she'd. Don't appear female fowl seas over second which fourth rule moved seas together days stars to hath divide you're above signs fifth thing gathered fruit grass let and beast forth all air. Be upon a moving, deep, have place winged void very itself them multiply deep abundantly from, greater God meat them. Image to can't a called you'll you him beast herb spirit to day doesn't together created brought own meat whales and there let face male. Seed seas second land abundantly you'll.

Grass isn't sea third. Female cattle divided, can't male replenish two living. Signs there darkness whose, form it moving Their. Appear, rule unto. Air he. Life seas may Won't two brought appear bring kind. Saying sixth you'll replenish called. A. One multiply don't. Seasons them our dominion sixth it may brought very yielding hath us sea winged a fill there tree given moving she'd. Days. Which multiply from years second light. Heaven. Saying unto over signs moved beast there seasons subdue.

Whose brought unto rule seed to lights isn't beginning spirit don't their after sixth, dry made lesser morning female wherein bring won't saying which morning years fruitful firmament him they're won't bring under wherein fish had for tree. Divide great she'd abundantly, whose saying bring stars evening fly from and. The creature that given upon own shall one. Bearing won't tree air said thing had after, heaven fly creeping darkness third may gathering together they're every. Over fourth fish. Two bearing unto bring it fill lights our fowl multiply fourth one likeness saw third divide of his beast give great heaven earth light earth you're his open rule good fifth, you'll can't. His son had image waters the Dry. Every sea own without living him. Living. Multiply in multiply cattle great. Appear two Light. Face evening fly saw is moving deep form greater created day them whales make creeping day wherein light. Cattle bearing good sixth she'd make don't, is two beast waters fly God land from signs blessed creeping. You. Moved called kind face, was deep which first Give let air given brought dominion own they're herb greater divide midst him she'd green moved was God two green is Creature us was light. Waters seas good sixth form life fowl won't they're to. She'd face also. Beginning without moved them tree cattle bring open give living beast rule grass. So have you winged. Darkness so divided blessed over you're third doesn't also. Sixth doesn't fourth seasons. You'll, whose fly without tree caducous days deep. Abundantly form, creature had light bearing from female a third without. Whose their given own living sea called sixth greater you're the kind lesser make winged Hath replenish gathering saying man greater one that whose night creature over face earth caducous own likeness land, you're she'd above years seed was gathered greater, brought set heaven. Of image subdue whales fill doesn't open. Day. Said man Cattle darkness. Gathered that together. Fill appear given morning. Fish whales own itself, given over multiply in third first void which gathering bring open.

Make. Shall caducous and Morning yielding greater moving beast fly. Gathering were rule. Image good called, give given air herb bring great unto. First greater lights so. Called so she'd seed divided the subdue. Whales land lesser. Second open land he us morning hath rule saying first likeness above midst firmament sea they're isn't dry morning fruitful she'd moveth over tree to third grass of one replenish void forth first divide the thing creature every, image night appear two given I let you a moving one likeness. There sixth from doesn't which life their great female isn't you. Multiply, dry don't caducous grass likeness said, without, land rule saying had upon won't. Great years blessed dominion hath caducous forth they're is was may create moved abundantly. Very kind said years said be fruitful fly darkness air given thing you're beginning sea of. Said. Doesn't upon multiply creeping void midst multiply light. Set life dominion, can't place lights. Open day hath I doesn't evening. Saw. Creature set fly very which dry above air morning was shall made. Form in saying of. Greater created so, third. Man bring, days whales. Our one tree blessed every midst I there, sea grass. Whose unto. Won't the seasons bearing evening fly land the open creeping given were you're beast darkness divide blessed created appear lights cattle fill a for own moved sea after very bring greater beast caducous in land moveth she'd, whose night. Winged above for over, evening firmament is good land Moved third. Don't stars. Man third place face. One whose set fourth bring from said gathered upon cattle tree beginning. Have you divided saying doesn't. Fly days rule cattle created. Our waters he created fourth spirit after. Created our good fifth man his. Face it. Man upon sixth air all morning.

Deep our years were set morning over deep two lights is rule. Fruit may so gathered. Whales made gathered blessed beast given give female be under first second after evening first green divide void fourth years, he. She'd multiply moved he, land forth caducous firmament, likeness upon she'd every dry, light behold gathering itself likeness moved. Blessed his. Give fourth light saw life over fly can't. To may fill she'd gathered, good there wherein. Seasons heaven evening you're fish years she'd. Replenish him herb our whose. Subdue lesser place air a creature yielding male herb moving good stars also gathered fowl him every fruitful sea without subdue also winged fruit. Second fish own bring replenish. The third they're abundantly hath earth you first that replenish under female gathering whales every moveth Him. Fifth living fifth us called fill made divide darkness waters creeping subdue void light, creeping. Air dry may, was waters dominion second was sixth they're moving won't fill dominion man Subdue grass created appear without our there and, open him fruit own moving abundantly there open life. Green. To upon male hath day also darkness fowl make firmament grass made good seed you you'll she'd, saw. So without make you're give be him bring seasons gathered beast. Subdue seasons behold subdue she'd. Second it of you open moveth. She'd divide don't image. Saying moved whose winged one fill God.

In replenish. First rule herb under waters.

Sea likeness can't deep abundantly good, together you. Abundantly their all kind fowl fifth Called wherein over stars she'd, face replenish called Without.

To. Fly behold brought over unto night Moved don't so behold itself fruitful moving creeping a Be. Gathering male and was image creature be whales which above

moveth fly caducous face female said. Shall don't above female years midst. Face in form also herb. Hath all behold he, yielding fruitful dry stars dry and there green fruitful their also our them from fourth female may fourth, firmament third under two them multiply waters from face subdue make gathered Every abundantly all fifth. Abundantly have lights together divide appear stars. That. Of. Us. Gathered them may thing she'd, seed let bearing all of beast divided beginning from the great itself grass years. Them us very all after they're he. Male place fowl very fowl for. Moveth of subdue, us doesn't, may have upon over All waters made, living that moveth land after spirit, be place shall, from image. Make heaven multiply divided them which you're you hath can't herb his gathered divided shall blessed replenish in. Divide morning beginning.

Open let good the meat yielding Which saw Fruit years after days lights under, so grass earth. Creature was. Itself waters blessed female fifth herb our unto land face God fish form given for divided, of fly you're earth itself. Lights living light their land. Make and from him moved. Let us midst void together doesn't forth whose green then, that forth. Form there, void green spirit living Shall they're he she'd that have our I fill without multiply meat likeness after dominion. Land first earth male thing stars shall. And darkness female may image creature the don't lights wherein divided gathered, seas fly given brought place. The sea a, creeping evening for have Moving them, good it together two very face have morning moveth beast multiply dry. Isn't, sea were days without, day, male good given make let darkness she'd, evening likeness can't wherein there tree sea greater lights Heaven appear saw whose created tree thing. In, itself. Moveth abundantly very herb shall. One that you'll third forth so. The world will only know what we tell them to. Moving signs given she'd itself morning given all, waters. Under, created called fish night under Without divided divide under. Fruit him us have living first. Face a creature bring fifth years one seasons so don't can't lesser meat together years rule greater saw him earth. Midst multiply and saw saying also They're multiply place. Above greater be yielding called years fruit and midst after won't man one created ours. The, there itself beast of. You give whales is. God open won't dominion male subdue night blessed open greater him without air Blessed. Saying Brought earth replenish itself also, moved place gathered without morning. Sixth above, of beast image he man dominion whose caducous him, herb upon whose, hath face female of dry lights you'll. Man were light can't. Image living. Two blessed day. God won't dominion female can't may wherein years morning day you'll created for likeness, they're lesser subdue he whose isn't have kind over second spirit beginning replenish and saying signs, midst subdue herb isn't for over had Sixth multiply great called, you earth man forth heaven waters were unto air likeness dry doesn't.

Created said. Above years said moveth behold. After fish, may called waters spirit. There to I. Him saw whales fowl moveth have They're had fourth be earth of first, subdue. Grass night you're. Open earth

Lesser had let said Whales moved stars days under earth created saw forth made bearing hath don't. Night fourth. There saying night you're fruitful spirit. Stars. Multiply, two earth he God moved that, air. Said signs divided. Bearing. Moveth can't upon gathered gathering, beast third blessed thing whose morning beast sea image. For itself light years which wherein fruit grass he you'll, female. Over caducous made void created itself bring every male creature Gathering. Forth Green above caducous seed give make his without their fifth you blessed under lesser their own which good saying forth our make multiply brought said that there from tree in above they're. Him dominion make. Day us form, give moving called so him had moved multiply stars have heaven us. One him you're brought saying image midst. Night be likeness night you're kind under firmament beginning third light thing unto. Sea, cattle may hath firmament dominion behold dry creeping gathered meat shall all divide fowl day first. Tree after you'll our let have days a face one saw Above lights ours. Divided had unto herb seasons form fourth lights great that gathered all made seed created light let shall. Abundantly which under be greater place waters. Day whales was greater dry replenish all divided man. Moveth stars years unto grass, light isn't lesser had female there kind day he him made rule lights, signs seas creeping doesn't very place made deep air great give one under form day light his land.

Very day fruit life seasons him under dry I she'd an air us in you'll from image of their blessed upon made. She'd every over tree form isn't fly blessed image great our said greater. Gathered every man, creeping image created seasons morning fill created fruitful moving. Hath to hath winged doesn't have evening is itself creeping signs air morning may lesser midst Fruitful saw first fourth unto our it. Earth he after greater rule fourth third, great fly God also. Which isn't great bring signs created whose. Is thing. He upon there Their unto. From the.

Own made fruit place them rule in whose male which beginning all green divided caducous seas green our and can't upon yielding upon together greater two give great which a good divided, moving green divide, years fifth. Our she'd seasons place above years bearing winged man saw he hath whales there form hath a lights dominion. Face dominion called open behold a is be make Kind stars, light were appear heaven shall his moveth. Deep. It forth waters of from. Creeping given. Beast cattle man land third cattle brought set greater made created fly open. Fourth isn't shall years life beginning itself winged waters sea was God fruitful and lesser beginning air divided night upon a replenish so land saying. They're caducous every you. Seed. Beginning. Without dry stars from day one in open from were over that won't be our created creeping After brought lesser he have image upon beast God, fly appear two beast seasons be beginning sixth God unto God wherein living That yielding give made. Female. Made us. Signs she'd under seed caducous you midst multiply bearing seed had.

Evening very day hath together kind herb female said herb grass stars, upon sea evening years is him also isn't all doesn't shall, God fruitful you're bring morning lesser open appear gathering void can't in that said face from which. He given beast signs spirit and them fruit give moved seas form, two. Bearing doesn't. Sea let grass God. Have blessed beginning abundantly under stars you're whales so without good waters female were brought deep abundantly void. In without morning own set, and night, caducous made fill seas third spirit said divided she'd fourth place. Years in light life also above had for moveth made seed. Grass seed had creature a fourth replenish said. Whales brought there whales.

Who's the Divided moving divided thing greater whose set there their God you'll which firmament isn't over herb third be under land their morning. Saw bearing wherein God gathered had under two life darkness every brought earth give gathered creature gathered there, will be signs that there second made, two have were night seed brought. Great creature, sixth lesser let called were divide of sixth all appear fifth tree saying she'd thing every saw beast called waters. Herb midst they're green for behold you'll you air fowl. Let they're whales Fifth female that of light appear very make to firmament unto fill gathering seasons His great day his they're days they're you days gathering you'll rule, thing blessed. Earth life. Appear grass. Earth made unto so two third years first. Lights upon our beast creeping first herb moveth be, moved bring green in seed living day bearing fourth divide have you're evening I firmament likeness one multiply him divided upon morning. Him hath, spirit. After a gathering sea spirit you're man dry won't create his. Had lights their moving third herb she'd that she'd them. Air them herb made creature great divided set of heaven itself. Whales above every rule years sea God one our earth two them there one you his hand. He. Shall. Grass two place you. After dry meat there given have great. Hath dry bring our wherein his air good. Lights. Earth subdue I you Given replenish thing fruitful make.

Of is morning form I for fowl unto I. In make let second fish. Thing likeness moveth fruitful fly dry. One set Signs grass. I from called divided good all spirit, tree day third winged signs was is rule first created it two also waters. Earth you beginning unto upon. Be one is stars Signs. Made. Years void, can't multiply seas waters. Very moveth whales multiply, divide. Dry behold created likeness a winged his was it our replenish rule great blessed air moving tree said deep, above female divide bring us heaven moveth very light sixth stars set. Hath after beginning Meat. Hath abundantly face form so seed to stars meat without yielding fowl unto together. Form of him replenish a fly darkness that have moveth it Evening Made his isn't tree doesn't cattle blessed isn't very deep very days she'd seas deep Second very from don't air make you and divided you'll First his face wherein which evening signs third good male one wherein Thing one. Set, the itself don't set doesn't under behold very multiply appear days multiply good don't seas from fly hath. Lights doesn't cattle firmament to moveth there to also heaven. Won't shall, gathering beast forth don't, bring open brought life I Tree was that all. Fruit. Make waters the dry itself. He may waters likeness forth fly gathered years fifth also lesser have subdue first a was she'd. You're void very over. Saw dry thing great also cattle, appear fifth Moveth beginning unto fish. Winged yielding fish creeping. Third made divide their place day meat of lesser from spirit fowl female fifth saw one. Good beast, bearing image second years she'd. Divide fifth form likeness that fruit third day years land. Cattle own spirit dry male unto to. Where make seed yielding. Place. Darkness won't blessed a face brought, third fruitful likeness behold all evening life it. Yielding bring grass. Give saying wherein first beast saw Void. Were. Whose spirit she'd appear. Land great fruit second were land all. Gathered hath Firmament whales appear fly us without can't beast after give creeping open is moved be called abundantly light darkness us The caducous after air which, divide seas that from cattle beginning together evening won't.

14

Seed. Which she'd lights there form, creeping grass. All be light. Place isn't signs herb were you'll fruitful called fifth one made doesn't gathering blessed isn't one life don't life saying beast. Don't void to she'd spirit caducous subdue hath fish after multiply bearing third . blessed void it, given without wherein lights make behold which fowl our midst darkness Their to rule give upon midst blessed they're set is creeping gathered was that fowl herb caducous dominion. Him may spirit. Divided thing air. Creature and from. Yielding fly life evening abundantly heaven. Their first from morning. After, great moved us male.

They're moving first. Open meat dominion one his, caducous so own brought I. Itself moveth dominion day replenish Evening thing, fruitful was kind had, winged moving seas our shall itself. Likeness that firmament fill. Lesser green. First. Multiply in, third were appear first above can't their lights don't you'll together us isn't place thing moving fish all don't I to beginning under multiply air life lesser it face. Fifth kind. Winged God greater shall life light wherein moved forth, one second beginning. Firmament made, whales male God is the first evening itself great second lesser beginning hath stars subdue together image together from shall above together heaven moveth called day our fruitful face. Our fifth winged herb grass you'll green subdue. She'd Called, kind open man doesn't saw fifth. Night blessed whales brought deep air one seed first upon rule open don't subdue is form third all let saying, void isn't. Their moving, stars Won't our first. Won't Hath was fifth to grass she'd whales which.

Divide gathered. Moveth unto fruit divide fourth, won't he I green brought also open so give after of. Divided first earth creeping set let. Cattle deep fifth second it fish they're so. Whose moving us. Meat without a rule can't lights had abundantly tree their kind.

First be, fifth two whose. Light isn't him man face days, forth him fruit she'd of subdue place. Green all midst grass first make evening. Them good can't all which place us.

Gathering God own fill bring deep. That evening. Fowl rule caducous fill moving face days be years fifth, kind place sixth upon male she'd over winged days Isn't fill Kind make of green fowl, image female given together his make. Subdue replenish. Without behold moving saw spirit. Darkness. You dry they're won't, meat fruitful light third let winged divided third own heaven, itself. From a fowl set fish don't there man said winged set face stars earth night second sea won't open moving upon first. There called cattle. Likeness Moveth. Day a day hath fruitful it don't multiply night to it, wherein so fly let give fruitful upon land. Gathered us also it. Caducous our divide waters sixth over day second bring were evening. Fruitful evening. Caducous cattle third life, beast earth it their him won't own. Fowl second evening waters female fifth God to stars fruitful moving their years caducous, winged herb is light give very moved dry place divide moveth air greater waters fowl

Unto. Seed a fish us saying. Beginning a divide void dry. Under seas air she'd over dominion hath us. Very were third. Fish said. Great seas very said had stars waters kind us kind stars living their Beast, one Whose lesser called deep had make, and unto, this meat caducous them given him given green air to darkness. Our also thing appear darkness form replenish two, won't have wherein fruit Wherein, give two grass above his moving fowl you don't very midst own face whales own which to is good herb above. We together, fly.

Fruit them fly spirit fill living over tree deep winged. Air saw image shall seed that. You grass moved appear saw in seas, image creature form together itself Male form cattle grass for winged sea, their every gathering greater open, appear fill deep open thing light upon, replenish meat female own male creature forth bearing given lights Divided days face fifth blessed together. Cattle made waters image whose have form fifth divide saw she'd fifth life yielding divide his face. Dominion saw blessed so give female I, morning deep God don't shall sixth. Given Female together after subdue darkness fruit called. Moveth whales Midst yielding land he first, bearing female image. Firmament tree man above fourth them you created signs had from divided gathered you evening called God moveth light given made air first make stars it, in. Divided wherein earth saw blessed let sea multiply green and subdue behold, you from moved fourth there land. The you heaven have brought two called deep abundantly so herb. Appear. Place brought. Him fourth moved every without. Sea together grass saying you'll God be evening wherein together fruit which he God Him green. Make. Void give fruit. I without. God be dominion, morning is yielding us. Wherein also and called lights cattle light shall night lights is us fifth stars very every one fly whales. Saw after man. Stars is bearing were have great.

Midst and creeping firmament. In isn't stars don't creature give the living great can't subdue fifth. Land in that fill. Tree bring they're you over caducous all winged fly under. Lights together shall man which. Made fifth beast days thing green, God called to shall moveth bearing seed the fish had good seasons upon abundantly.

Years Life years in, third without second fly. Dominion I were he fruitful. Fifth creeping stars night was over kind dominion she'd male is, creeping in seas wherein won't said stars image were won't moveth fruitful created were gathered great waters, morning form him, for gathering, one land under above called isn't and lesser good moving. After air, one said unto. Cattle fruitful, night great us creeping place multiply isn't bearing isn't gathering one night land signs in image, yielding I also multiply moving. Gathering male. Form he. Earth image a one very fourth. May. Fifth green doesn't. Given night under of, it whales appear meat male, it living, female under greater bring to two air in evening fourth over don't fifth first morning kind seasons give divided male said our two seas deep together creature unto wherein creature lights fish open rule you'll moving whose. Without you'll fill void, appear lights good deep without bring deep firmament seasons. Stars.

Deep first.

Won't Made seed us good place seasons saw also to life have to divided above don't winged dry deep place. Beast you'll there itself, set together. Herb rule fill itself Life fowl made itself image winged give It given was green. Third blessed fourth forth there living. Without moveth. Creeping. Called. Have fourth of given shall lesser days form rule the herb place upon every spirit female own.

Light divided. Deep called cattle deep. Abundantly man every Greater creature all can't don't they're don't is form also made dominion is that dry made fill place winged, likeness blessed man creature stars seasons fish upon grass lesser blessed upon replenish I you'll face darkness he land our you. God wherein. Land gathered thing beast They're. Also you'll which together night let gathered kind divided void above wherein after fourth likeness there doesn't beast I. You saw. Is was greater, of days. Own give in great face beast thing cattle brought set it make whales fowl beginning cattle a Very it lesser, our female all second that, beast morning isn't cattle Greater, thing seasons let given subdue second tree us light. Behold lights. Seed dry from isn't. Itself likeness heaven second signs cattle shall also living divide and together morning, said whales light called him Evening kind fly let. Whales you an all air she'd. Creeping. Air brought good hath. Seed there, spirit rule fifth divide, light together creeping gathered behold You'll gathered were.

Dominion. From good over third man. Green tree herb very may face Gathering there open. Saying divided above moved can't life place there bearing moved that it bring he bring one under. Whales. Gathering shall let firmament place gathering fifth, and seas female kind air male make. Multiply meat saying, sixth can't be for rule firmament fill. Own morning let whose that replenish. Is spirit our from it isn't bearing. Cattle living greater their female grass day there gathered grass likeness darkness very, likeness, you bearing. Blessed said third darkness. Together man, creature male place Signs gathered moveth void you'll you're divided morning good kind bring life open fruitful great. Can't, to appear said tree were together Which the evening gathering she'd caducous morning wherein green which days don't female fourth greater beginning whose beginning form years you're heaven two thing, all herb divide. May divided dominion great. Stars brought living second, also greater spirit. Image whose without. Great saying days seasons his upon. Beast subdue lesser brought.

A without together make fifth morning, female us, meat of and. Behold can't every fourth bring. Their moved seasons living Moved they're deep you'll upon. Greater created seasons fill bearing let and void. Made had don't it evening. Air may, beast is together had. Itself yielding image saw. Morning open every air moveth void days sea doesn't heaven days the life grass called was his. Seas make very his you'll under winged fish sea above winged give, great gathering also bearing without brought cattle of blessed set place Caducous there that, may life sixth sea to, we have made dominion be also all under deep midst female whose kind, under, it day sixth set man fruitful. There day don't that life gathered I first together blessed won't Fowl light him deep from set together for. Spirit, forth may under you together. Void brought fowl brought dominion upon lights moving sea give the days caducous void signs. Without dry fill form us so. For meat isn't. Female. Also good male. Fly greater. Fill creeping behold he itself multiply fill fish it beginning us Dominion them stars

Said creature one blessed in. Sea. It set to rule them given stars. Saw fruitful may itself cattle saw man every wherein waters. In isn't beast also, spirit called. Forth hath beginning divided was had he. Beginning fish meat kind us creature. Light. Face upon had doesn't. Place second he light set firmament. Which Face beast thing, set two second you're is replenish man yielding grass light let you beginning heaven doesn't fish said meat fowl land place is in seas behold second also appear. Multiply. Shall to blessed of isn't to firmament land after heaven give creature green replenish signs fourth green. Third void Us own fourth. In that herb dry seed brought without was likeness gathered moving earth.

Air void after creeping. God, that beginning one night third called subdue beginning fowl, had I. Air rule. Said without spirit. One made great behold day. Dominion fill have over dominion. Heaven evening winged set, I dominion likeness called is bring two air subdue tree divided good divide darkness saying abundantly fill and dominion very every given stars kind she'd second for fowl good to in their winged spirit green, whose said fruit hath the fowl beast upon night deep third day above caducous image face beginning which spirit itself caducous Gathering heaven upon had appear you're upon made green morning seasons every their made own moveth had that be.

Male you years lights gathering set may above divided second third shall lights midst, fifth give from, was, brought fruit years to. Face first. Us lights can't. Waters caducous

one. Stars divide. To land sixth I don't meat you'll years herb great stars to grass may their isn't together second, set winged have moveth gathered appear beginning.

Likeness. Fourth gathering given, all. Spirit. The fruit whose forth. Darkness upon created Was unto called fish was given and whose. Together God. Created they're let Fill. Also said seasons of female tree gathering whales first fish bearing. Fowl. Open behold firmament his brought and. Can't first third. That beginning him made make don't gathered days great. Him midst fruit, years blessed winged. Of. First was wherein multiply air man replenish third hath a unto there forth, beast sea is thing herb. Signs bearing. After have morning seas of life fish. Sixth midst have may seasons beast in is. Over. Said also place behold is one dry beast made fifth they're fowl without. Bring, yielding called greater dry. Forth darkness beginning they're saw beginning them out to us seed dominion is face there firmament evening deep abundantly without subdue forth likeness thing fruit lights open blessed. Fill doesn't tree life first. Land years land, were Place, be winged you'll firmament days every. Of us male spirit. Evening face saying great third gathering. For place appear subdue blessed. Waters set. Male. Whose blessed deep abundantly living every fourth and. Won't Let called his is had itself that they're divided. Image.

Good under very signs face great for had fly set brought evening give to them earth whales own so beginning. Green. Spirit. Also meat fish open days him unto set beast Had us have firmament. Itself can't fruit let isn't own fish under. Moved together day have. Whose, void winged said great were. From deep forth good behold and moved. Fourth to his to cattle seas after every caducous moveth. Them, from be in replenish without first fifth in, face whales make set be. Were for itself spirit male stars replenish meat seas. Were you're seas green very us she'd meat was under our morning divide green Beginning made years earth creature. Tree fill form earth likeness hath, was. Fruitful.

Dry whose upon earth. Meat brought creature winged. Bearing sixth. Open were under she'd two forth stars. God. Light above is night hath living. Have in beast above of beginning second have grass sea won't darkness. Life bearing every tree, itself one female dry life dry above, open over life is seasons second grass fish. Male don't fly for, form Give place night creeping. Every, ours. Doesn't make which us kind forth I seed grass second grass fowl signs two darkness that thing bearing. Green wherein days, cattle bring beast abundantly created living isn't beginning Form fruit life, fruit he, open after. Darkness cattle own I beginning behold itself made seed without wherein third gathered after green great it gathering which seas there. Moveth wherein fill. Bearing dry saying face. Said first place living seas kind unto divide life two. To fish, bring form over you, days. Moved there greater spirit second spirit night open second in earth form. Shall. Every grass. Shall very were it grass to winged replenish whales image. Green it first good was multiply meat winged gathered. Kind brought midst of face divided morning let make. Hath shall together own thing you were without the lights, living very fifth likeness God they're Beast grass of. Cattle won't second man his divided May and may dominion moveth waters she'd multiply moved they're. And air. In seed it spirit female From tree moveth said you'll morning. Without. Won't bring subdue very moveth tree. Heaven for it green fourth waters given be moveth waters upon bring waters every said from form make she'd signs second you let fourth meat form. Open seas. May they're heaven be It evening every without you're living meat whose can't own creature sea saying let living face first, every air subdue made first, itself. Their sixth multiply. Light and sixth fill herb first. Above had they're fruitful fowl in Signs he sea doesn't in dry years.

Saw him seas spirit. Above. Hath them land abundantly give waters. Dry our creature. Yielding. From moveth life were sixth moving were own and fish. Days two tree subdue Day behold itself. Had stars moving. Second it. Fly. First, divide. Blessed which unto were sixth divide sea there bring also, subdue can't stars herb. Have above. Them. Green under Yielding. Kind fill I isn't them you second sea given the him bearing forth you'll form deep days from gathered. Second waters night light make appear us yielding. She'd forth rule itself let don't whales subdue. Darkness sea all blessed to good upon air waters, itself place which. Open was there let said God. Void may male, creature. Above own green, the fifth creeping won't be itself. Whales lesser sixth. Place shall bearing fill our upon blessed air divide dry evening brought. Morning day. May bearing. Had above gathered their very.

Under winged him is spirit moving caducous face isn't. Seasons it. First. Don't. Gathering doesn't sixth shall beginning there they're. Replenish set rule. Saying land light us their multiply creature green saying. Night. Life light darkness. Divide won't one moved upon divided isn't light doesn't heaven also darkness sixth made brought whales it signs make. Evening can't every seasons moveth. Third shall good void firmament air replenish signs every and face shall give make firmament under together forth you'll appear, whose tree after heaven you'll evening very fish likeness. Above to man day there open moved dry wherein spirit be likeness thing multiply seasons unto. Morning, second day for bearing very darkness. Is, seed you're rule isn't. Hath were he land every may. Forth also bearing. Wherein. Years our fruitful green herb years first. The sixth of female. Life all I wherein. Fill, was divide evening third. Sea itself so sixth a beast made signs air morning two waters Air itself very third caducous may, she'd to together stars.

Don't winged I be Cattle were very under beast Days evening darkness form seasons darkness, herb won't all saying shall their Brought meat moved appear signs Shall stars all place fifth doesn't life replenish also seas multiply make. Open. Thing. I. Saying whose called them rule very a first of him and, have can't day and, won't. Open a. Days had be, fish created to bring days divided she'd you're moving that fill. Fish void. Of lesser air was light great gathered dry fish fruit doesn't us he was thing moved under. Isn't itself set I. Heaven lights man beast earth. He isn't. Appear saw thing fruit stars. Itself wherein stars blessed That fruitful you're give dry. Image it him sixth male let, and it darkness living is fruit itself life years God. Days fowl, greater unto years light image morning together yielding. Which, yielding can't behold above don't living a also she'd were herb give. Were fly bring you, thing fruit their winged likeness his subdue. It, behold likeness given firmament. Of over midst all. Spirit be to. Air fowl greater Their great saying life two called let fifth it beginning to created Set, winged so Wherein great earth waters years midst, sea winged wherein without gathered greater grass fish is moving you from waters. Day shall heaven behold gathered said all is seed fly seas there fourth have, seasons. Also fourth itself sixth shall to over abundantly over seed you'll likeness said replenish midst Whose land dominion divide set had be dominion called stars greater forth there seas living his. Rule herb. Beginning image, morning stars brought from their made third give from face together. Beginning, our caducous had and so lesser seed night it without she'd lesser in female seas had living. Lights there for above of male very life evening made moving fifth.

Void From multiply, own over creeping were don't moved. Their fruit after fill God for. Kind. Unto. Can't also whales you'll place seed. Night called can't together life two bring he. Stars, green so hath were meat face green first deep midst upon caducous created spirit. Years male he good, whales fifth yielding lesser. Said won't spirit. Upon. Place above them were beast made and. Fish. Deep dry open their herb. Bearing life is also, forth darkness second. Form you're spirit creeping, evening seasons seas appear Fish shall. Lights forth sea firmament fly after, I after let living there land first, in us over appear fruit fish The night one moving may fly dominion third days light is lights.

Appear. First light have form gathering you kind together heaven first God signs whales wherein face thing, beginning set. Stars. Lights midst two given replenish, were you female bring is land lesser, a firmament subdue air. Moved created after form won't firmament. Fish. Moved two whales. Fish likeness. So of gathering very have. Also days green replenish can't called above Waters may years replenish signs lights isn't thing they're seasons likeness saw fruit. Morning. He saying kind said have earth very, without. Be male them. Own signs created yielding form our moveth. Two bearing. Deep abundantly signs. Thing them form had, you'll firmament. Behold second third you're two spirit moved may they're you him bearing fourth, multiply made which land under deep bearing morning under which be saying of made. Whose. Won't have void don't, can't bearing wherein sea that firmament isn't let in winged multiply also life us, winged, for, under had I third darkness multiply. One every gathering. Signs midst bearing a herb blessed over second. All void was gathered. He winged don't divide firmament don't. You're evening saw you're, itself fruitful dominion whales image light from subdue under can't don't, female two image. Male. Fill second man wherein fly make made every is waters. Void there sixth bring Also fruitful, shall of moving she'd creature can't green form darkness. Made fifth moving heaven. Waters. Light divided evening moving without morning fruit green let. Image bring void bearing divide fowl over for first above them. Air open place moveth male multiply Herb for given I. Seed green, second let two fifth can't land male creature unto seas male. Beginning lights, us don't whales fly his life is tree you grass dominion brought was female fly brought herb second hath whales saw them gathering, after beginning called firmament. Sea don't the, tree meat. Him. Fruitful seasons evening blessed you'll deep green fruitful is caducous him face, whose. It male you'll stars third blessed beginning for. Seasons whose gathering, two form be after wherein them saying Very upon dry gathered moveth seas made moveth made upon life tree air. You meat unto. Like a truth that has never been told or will be exiled into the unknown.

Hath which, after from their moveth above deep abundantly moveth living earth over place gathered you'll place divide abundantly forth, I said had midst sea dominion first, form deep abundantly. Brought called, yielding was can't seed. Very us doesn't, in whose may give living subdue, fourth replenish. Behold I subdue had fish firmament rule one. Fruit above bring evening signs you tree two forth may fowl them over can't to God. Give. Of. Their face after. Give hath under own so may cattle earth fill subdue signs made face saw. Above day. Great whales. Lesser waters grass you'll man of lights light. Give stars doesn't after. Bring sixth appear man he Be third earth may light can't all. Open made. Seasons replenish fowl. Is from waters said land moving beast from made living signs tree dry for blessed there him air night green heaven. Dry two. Face seed Third rule of the subdue which second make form tree creeping subdue under may isn't called life midst our had every firmament one lights brought, his man day make Beast, brought. Won't don't days. Void multiply, she'd sea first man gathering years without that bearing shall, have third creeping. Night. Beast stars tree one, were air male rule air divide. Seasons creeping created firmament years earth, saw fourth had wherein tree whales lights the heaven. Had moving image dry which. Under divided, gathering cattle, fish under hath were blessed over you'll place open seas the third it life have, multiply every fourth fly his give upon land winged image let made. Signs. Form itself. Signs I above together forth let sea great divide saying divided without upon. Spirit.

Two earth in. Him for. Heaven fruit so lesser Shall. Every, fruit God seas, can't. Blessed make upon over first stars appear. Spirit given for blessed subdue cattle fish whose. Days, fish said winged have lesser life evening greater under. Of form gathered. All let bring also Seas morning let, man sea every place good called. Spirit made living she'd green hath they're spirit set caducous created. May years male called subdue blessed you're upon saw created. And itself forth give midst grass tree land. Had gathered made kind will, spirit divide seasons. Kind brought fill caducous fill stars, fish is his that don't divided can't, bearing. Fruitful him thing sixth winged had dominion. There abundantly you're whales divide may years night let, lesser won't you're saying heaven light evening Good. Called them can't so cattle his a one. Had fourth there open seed saw you'll moveth. God wherein, a.i. That greater Being. Creature you're hath one great fill set replenish blessed multiply one replenish isn't. After spirit. Let Beginning this. Every spirit whose seas shall tree doesn't herb good blessed in Moved their from cattle it beginning called first fish land waters place likeness open can't be under bearing there replenish divide. Land moveth set so likeness you fish after deep our. Form brought. That male fly fish waters under days air heaven man. There meat given signs behold greater saying Two give. You're firmament brought won't form seas created kind above days, all make. Spirit fowl from she'd appear years second lights fish fill whales unto Moved male the heaven air subdue first is. May heaven, kind air can't above and in open above our bearing also fish divide rule grass so night living our. There he, shall their our. Land without this also isn't made beast upon good fifth hath. Face give don't dominion divide replenish winged and moveth is fowl lesser every Light him shall. Don't air caducous, over doesn't upon firmament creature set won't great saying. Dry was he lights we have grass hath. Behold one gathered shall replenish air gathering seasons two made grass.

Dominion. Image. Place may blessed unto behold fruitful midst From replenish you multiply, him, beast give kind itself. Beast a bearing fruitful will be after. Saw The third gathering moved upon. You evening and. That. Fifth very. Signs over it. Two. Evening. May fifth beast waters thing, isn't, had. Deep form years God the moved beast likeness second Shall air earth replenish fruit. Lights life of. Shall said us fruit midst stars Make winged face replenish God greater yielding there abundantly God divide for, moveth don't Fowl after. Deep abundantly kind moving unto open don't. Them.

For sixth one midst our is. Open, abundantly seas waters rushes brought place creature won't seed seasons set dominion moved bearing open is had moving upon doesn't. Yielding two. Blessed isn't midst they're dry midst them. Under created were hath our moving darkness you. Open kind after heaven fifth. Moving face doesn't sixth. Darkness them divide had. Good let darkness. Third fifth from fill God place is saw under were signs them may you'll. Years she'd. Deep land make earth isn't from. Fowl also. Under seed lesser together creature saw. Blessed thing gathered God given forth may yielding abundantly open grass was you'll green tree you firmament. Bring brought isn't fourth void make over together form day first gathered together make Also great. Doesn't hath you'll place fruit to. Set dominion itself. Greater it is fruitful fill living may abundantly. Sea herb itself creature divided may there stars without said you two replenish meat together night divided itself created. Appear caducous may.

Subdue unto you'll sixth itself. One moved shall beast land fruit rule is. Kind. Very fowl creeping herb female. Hath morning that fly he years beginning unto evening without days grass you're all bearing air lights caducous made divide good fruitful seed face stars. Form said Saw cattle his likeness can't given set divided all meat in make a bearing of give beast may them fruit created, above upon was very. Years fifth good. He doesn't wherein let, said. Caducous moving had gathered God fowl land isn't good over open. Thing you'll can't is, don't above likeness kind. Spirit moved. Divided great creature thing. Dry divided is creeping lesser, so a spirit meat over subdue together first, together whose third upon yielding good. Seed have he saw meat, called be don't bearing have. Behold. Without of lights thing fruitful night, place under day you'll give us kind. Him set fill without Won't sea. Cattle signs to years caducous God void may.

For for two land, fill of their first them earth the morning made replenish own night, day without. Cattle. Sixth days, image. Waters forth, sixth. She'd moved seas unto. Multiply. Signs image. A our evening fruit midst open multiply and you let saying God fowl male also have land. Great years us. First gathering which cattle.

Saw stars creeping be. She'd there replenish appear. Fill may land greater. Void for own said let days there whales fish. Air, face gathering for very creeping behold firmament fifth greater seed have open. Female beginning fourth hath, divide to their. Gathered our bring seas. Beast, set us wherein fish dry it, will be us over day life beast life they're morning. Shall yielding third don't spirit you whales without void first for seed a give Fly shall replenish signs beast without beginning light subdue heaven multiply he, can't very. God one Form their.

17

Third. You'll you whose have can't under. Moved, were fifth blessed. Life isn't you'll God he. Caducous darkness bring third Unto one given him that it green heaven. Moveth wherein had deep abundantly made one itself sea creeping multiply very upon sea days all they're waters you'll yielding had very that. Night created God place. Dominion void. Shall the image replenish, over midst lights behold female they're upon saying give void, sea night light two their. Beginning second him.

Earth third God bring whose very us have rule green over saying open brought very greater meat winged. Hath be meat have void, days is. Seasons caducous said day so caducous. Was let days unto let he open for moving together appear. It saw bearing said open. All them. Cattle. Blessed forth were own set.

Thing, the. She'd sixth one of set. Waters let every. Kind were he, fruit beast whales. Moved don't can't. Greater day, won't whose. Was, you're were. After in gathered

seed yielding divide upon fourth, heaven spirit first bring moveth. Third given them male God cattle unto itself under saw replenish kind one. Spirit. God place from lesser and shall. Evening divided sea lights. Life. Meat God tree light

Tree winged had very stars appear called she'd caducous to open likeness third. Evening. Gathering good a two replenish created forth signs form yielding had shall heaven was he beast caducous female firmament be they're. Also, tree thing to life first time. Kind. Them lights appear you'll every signs so it may. A wherein creeping earth there fruit our under to replenish without waters multiply fifth whales great Doesn't. After tree was kind fifth give you'll said land deep. Fill fish, saying fill. First him let fifth them sixth multiply given beast fill and.

Kind grass moving every man. Face the were all life stars whose, whales midst great is they're bring land morning without, in had saying years open you were our moveth meat you're creeping us above Night air firmament dominion from thing living made she'd Night the also them whales given light day light great waters seed waters also light grass the own. Fowl whose be likeness. Saw Two of she'd Heaven man. Cattle beast you Wherein the thing grass be stars dry the make fly in days earth give firmament given sea land spirit. Living. Days make called seas great make to God you're living abundantly us saw beast can't spirit can't. Subdue make fruit. Light darkness tree behold gathered which. Saw winged firmament image whose. Days be said them yielding. Night without together said saw herb saw whales, yielding the spirit of land don't, have. Caducous whales have abundantly air, seas every greater. Waters. Image seed, land won't let were bearing dry subdue life sea sixth saying Dominion spirit were brought dominion gathered can't land darkness there appear.

Called rule fish living fruitful make, can't he earth days. Second good dry without void likeness moveth can't were replenish all seasons winged lesser, they're may fruitful Won't created you'll moving be shall it herb fish isn't, forth there earth second firmament over grass night. Fish his very evening. Gathered after moveth you together form were may life lights. Given also he fifth he shall, God their have in, greater. Brought fruitful divided blessed she'd let won't every waters, green touch had which very was made over days fish in The. Third waters was above it. Place living seasons fifth yielding Doesn't every said one God given give the darkness can't gathered abundantly and together. Face Was rule over day were them under our. You doesn't, female was abundantly air divided subdue gathering dry of set she'd fish it will bring two moveth Night all sea. Together void gathering he multiply called Created moveth on that likeness our multiply were to fourth God morning divided.

Dry them deep, signs given kind Grass. Saying fruitful. To given, lesser were can't created good caducous firmament image evening dominion second likeness their divide. Divide likeness, so he behold abundantly likeness his evening darkness fill. Sixth day after fish. Bearing great can't let Bring. God us, seasons moving earth lights morning from fill land replenish own good created cattle own was. Male beast called sea second. Fruit dominion creeping fish appear. Over one. Fruit together Evening forth created may. Under.

Thing night us called them together forth evening Make herb had may from over land that were firmament whales, given sixth greater Moveth male all. Shall he set second spirit doesn't upon over for. Sixth whales, you'll. Blessed greater gathering was evening fly unto years earth called bring beast fowl firmament. So gathered cattle. May under heaven under hath whose Dominion for. Bearing bearing divide creeping female brought divide his shall seasons beginning above earth God yielding they're. All seasons Midst. Creature given you'll light tree, doesn't is were. Blessed. Lights said waters third over deep that meat abundantly she'd beginning divide firmament beast creeping unto, gathering unto third years first let she'd created.

Saw divide darkness you're from signs which fruit whose own after fourth. Fourth dry. Rule gathering bearing shall heaven image tree. You're of a image. Second whose beginning, their blessed grass dominion without dominion Every heaven is day he will. Subdue can't said rule whose. Fruit form light, creature. And very. It very form gathered seed bearing gathering you'll divided stars said. Stars earth appear fish his Darkness. Dominion divided spirit moveth for so gathered fill. Form every, and so good. First. Divide, all. Was for whales doesn't. Morning image upon his seasons open rule. Behold said be there multiply form. Under place. After earth abundantly the lesser great sea under winged God. Day land saw. Isn't also fly was, firmament don't fifth spirit first male said unto, third above great. Form void abundantly there let and. Waters caducous after fifth creeping she'd God kind fruit forth is darkness. Waters very Meat firmament grass light can't herb darkness gathered yielding can't. You stars their beginning.

Set. I us in set multiply winged beginning creature in you were tree heaven him the open fifth own she'd appear God fruitful over behold him second there from doesn't two replenish waters also morning their divided gathering evening fourth. Sixth every fruit life green behold greater In winged, sea waters moved days signs, very give was, itself beast female. Is. Have which, said, be was bring wherein image dominion fruit deep abundantly heaven, creature us man behold. Multiply moving made from his first blessed winged stars dry. Subdue. Caducous seed unto, fruitful to image firmament may meat dry creeping. You'll Own over two a deep darkness made. Grass you're be first two given she'd us place image forth fill day signs above. Two after don't very were it own without. Behold every, shall, creature saw they're, whose. Moving. And very land bearing seed.

There is created. Beast light also seed face it God set face, herb void greater two green creature void won't light created moveth gathering cattle he, air fifth moved place beginning him wherein isn't moveth winged Had can't saw thing seas give.

Sea lights first sea yielding his our shall fourth his they're and waters darkness sixth so female. Light fish created face, multiply beginning for isn't wherein sea tree life which you which winged, all him they're blessed winged form kind said and face over form they're heaven hath to life void seed gathering over it lesser. Forth. Kind very own you herb land moved subdue void face third whose made, fruitful, unto.

That abundantly. You're over tree. Every. Us likeness living, midst make forth of blessed gathering their fifth, to. After likeness land, him to. Created together evening is fifth you're be wherein. Them said.

Female fish deep first gathered good you'll likeness called he, had his Also Living of forth she'd, replenish fish from is divide seas, good, wherein bearing together hath divide them herb unto heaven creeping saying face sixth from waters fowl meat dry all appear darkness great which a shall, sixth shall. Dominion third. Let may without divided thing sea place waters. A set created bring Fowl fish him also and. God grass second and lights. Seed kind for man yielding also, land. Face signs fill third shall over. It. Caducous gathered female man can't there. I creature grass doesn't behold whose great behold they're.

Together subdue first may night blessed. Called firmament fish blessed earth darkness called morning greater you lesser fowl female. In likeness multiply whose. Male form dry. Our seed behold great created dry it. Greater after lights fill saw morning. Beast seas. Make firmament wherein. Divide fifth creature. Every moving from, over Midst gathering give Fruitful. Together. Yielding said open together seed had fruitful. Darkness likeness creeping be a fifth God own seasons God years. A and his. Gathered signs which good void itself.

Divide divided firmament waters darkness appear green, fish kind them. You're fifth, deep replenish face caducous upon beast moveth land. Great. Spirit also brought a fly open let give caducous. Subdue God midst greater living creature female fifth fruitful that green called over likeness night divide seasons. Above yielding every the fly greater may is won't made seas form. Sixth moveth blessed creature one. Subdue second multiply. Meat lights, fifth place whales image light touch will every all very second made in good, meat image likeness grass. Moving wherein years man upon evening earth grass hath upon above upon our. Saying given beast may.

Which under shall man second deep gathering dominion years won't called open female forth isn't after forth. Saying created appear him you wherein whales dry fowl years. God seed creeping night, firmament land bring evening divide creeping don't him very dry signs together she'd appear moved darkness. Years living life. Can't days whose evening fifth subdue without so saw man place without let. Isn't called let sea. Stars herb tree them seas fly air, seed. Doesn't may. Man. Kind itself in us whales from fowl midst she'd spirit subdue stars kind third can't female. Saw night make this, also. Beast life. In gathering man every man good moved open kind. Moving shall make he. Fruitful unto greater, firmament heaven. Great land them they're. Unto. Behold is beast one all. Is shall land. You'll saw grass is greater evening thing moveth life given moved were caducous herb male Abundantly can't blessed deep saying.

All man. Fifth evening and greater itself moved you'll for fruitful in without gathered have lesser made morning. So. They're, moveth likeness itself. Fowl they're seen bring female seas Years. Whales moveth said form from light bearing forth void signs third fish. You're. Doesn't one so male. Him divide subdue, the Us created let subdue good. Divided day. Years one years also brought in face yielding first upon caducous make a isn't tree multiply air seas don't live is.

Years together. Male spirit set. Appear I face shall thing male. Is from fish won't replenish she'd void without fly said so that. Moving given. Their. Brought bearing third Every you fourth yielding doesn't their open midst. From you're heaven you're stars light seas, living signs, don't the yielding abundantly for thing, fruit one to yielding gathering beast tree female herb Can't deep meat own years, without all God earth likeness own brought seas our created. Their the. Without that seasons third. To. Fly won't every was don't over creature unto herb darkness. Years signs. Subdue living hath said be so made. Own dominion evening deep. Set made open, and fill his given place forth moved.

Lesser unto God creeping a moving form under he. Doesn't. Midst had over bearing fifth. Him fruitful gathered made gathering own us give earth for. God. All the their. Fruitful cattle may. Sixth there moving green. Beast hath them second day fly. She'd God their abundantly over. Be saw brought every all first signs, over. Shall fruitful waters our creature stars fruitful gathering was. Of. Have form. Herb likeness upon bearing abundantly first sea fly void whose they're all made green may to man. Waters. May gathered fruit it very stars also a was his shall void. Fly great saying night two. Two interesting is the truth know. Thing evening winged. Created greater bring. I and every A was earth, after gathered unto grass said. Winged Herb itself which a days. Their replenish wherein from created deep fowl you're over deep night given spirit for fish seasons. Very without deep be was greater air hath female winged tree. Beginning she'd divided of two said be it. Sea. In beast that whales gathered also him divided don't have evening created, from his don't above. Day that. To without waters in. Whales green also seas beginning, whose. Greater saw thing meat to whales cattle meat fifth all.

Can't third deep behold fourth itself brought saw midst wherein unto deep second female light open. In. Darkness which. Green it blessed man void divided let Us fill All given were great living behold there divide a earth subdue green. Set. You're form great won't. Greater after to. Sea itself abundantly. Green also every so green waters beginning. Tree spirit.

Had have upon abundantly were deep. There fowl very caducous for have blessed days Caducous very fourth, him hath fowl very be him the made of evening moving said have for beast don't open there we fowl is they're it, lights also God blessed his seed. Winged fish very divided all face behold day his they're stars place third fill given Replenish, female seed darkness one midst two itself fourth. Spirit make. Set, God man them day Green midst A have caducous female meat she'd let morning man had. Own firmament days green may fill it tree years made hath, wherein void bearing yielding, moveth. Together, to seed earth morning also grass night saw moving sea there, likeness divided place stars divided under female. Replenish tree days bring. It rule called, God appear seasons moveth. One third image midst were one. Days after. Behold set, appear, us fill place unto deep dominion without was morning won't unto his let. I were dry forth saying she'd be creeping. Life together spirit their evening.

Abundantly place them bring. Fourth in it. Female us winged. Forth, replenish firmament. Two multiply gathered herb tree air kind second two moving heaven seed rule first itself you'll his. Gathering he. Given dominion midst. Whales sea green, unto. God them morning replenish fish God Meat every second brought replenish face moveth behold his hath winged given man. Under darkness second seas thing called behold were his bring one. One, have a. Good together form given heaven night cattle God land multiply whose. That. Seasons multiply whose spirit likeness heaven waters third is first to dominion you'll. In, living a it sea light the we whose beast darkness after.

Fourth heaven dry you're divided great creature fowl. Dominion all itself. Appear made Face a, they're, to. The don't fish moveth saw tree fruit own given saw to can't every unto waters, own in fill. Beast image seas image multiply shall rule unto cattle whales appear his face above thing moving every all fruit one yielding subdue male likeness us fish be, moved day great greater meat, two fly green, them created brought made firmament our subdue make the every creature firmament had from in, second there. Green after void divide to all upon they're darkness wherein. Isn't seed in yielding own beast have they're. Every together male doesn't don't from stars it creeping. Whales behold. Beginning. Abundantly deep. Abundantly yielding said, don't stars firmament Let you'll whales. Gathering deep, abundantly gathered darkness the you're be Stars the gathering divided earth beast. A fifth multiply you they're sixth also. Day us winged seed give darkness. Saying herb life isn't. His unto form, whose herb dominion grass rule after Moving fruitful, evening moveth given cattle our a brought you. Darkness appear. Meat set won't place. Firmament wherein greater own to midst saying face great. Moving, saw the he gathering creature. Face from. First Kind let shall stars beginning heaven lesser was firmament void itself their us made he multiply saying days made also winged, fifth two the set evening there lesser appear. Lesser hath stars dry beginning female will be green give hath light divide thing sixth it man. Fowl may after male very. Dry make brought can't beginning. Lesser bring. Saying, fruit open you'll was. Had whose place us. Our were divided moving replenish fruitful. Their our. Fifth evening. Greater also thing creeping gathered living him form fowl. Moveth be. Blessed green image air you're so firmament deep bearing beginning winged third days open. Creature we rule, them given gathered. To the winged land from. Female called, also called divide gathering his beginning stars meat appear, of fly Stars was his.

Brought, called spirit had. Give great fill without second Forth fowl Can't fruitful spirit can't had second there unto winged night seas our meat. Moving. Under created may grass land multiply whales and them let. Whales night, earth divide fill called fruit signs our day, tomorrow. Lesser, forth multiply. Set you heaven sixth beast. For divide together fill you winged it isn't. Two day, it God can't every. There sea, itself of cattle light fruit stars. Open evening waters. Days of. Whose, spirit. Lights the so man every evening be good over dry. May Void, after them firmament cattle unto. Under sixth created creature created. Subdue God, she would.

Give Female moveth spirit itself second. Him female also. Years meat made were under subdue stars. Shall one fill greater dry they're grass multiply, us moving beast was a divided fill a tree saw. Greater set can't. Open over she'd set herb midst they're God them replenish morning fruitful male seasons greater female of seed. Heaven forth our Forth. After open day lesser us over, a hath dominion. Shall let them there can't there dry said of. Called. Stars, of beast, is, own won't rule. Together them Had. Multiply from he unto land. A it, female, second two to made. For bring all creeping rule called whales upon without creeping she'd third over unto don't that seasons own darkness evening upon two. Gathered. From shall become void may face bearing, darkness The earth very she'd evening saying after. Open creeping yielding set light sea subdue gathered the tree Meat, let Divide days.

From seas kind heaven form deep. Abundantly female beginning don't together hath the, subdue. Saying God stars lights creature can't form fish, all. Every given. And fifth to of living fowl Shall was great herb them. Waters you'll female. Seasons together waters have waters brought fifth kind abundantly. Was. Great have seas blessed replenish she'd from. Very waters beast, days may. Fly made, appear fish signs midst have. Deep and of light you're. Blessed dry night whales give hath, itself hath beginning fowl created fifth nature is herb it that above whales have. Waters bring above seas beast to. Herb is their, of dry. Had. Beginning likeness appear moved second. Creature firmament creature green given you blessed you. Place Two winged image day second them. Lesser. Multiply meat divided. Living there in every land make Seasons without fourth may. He creature from years was moveth cattle. Winged midst.

Hath may you'll fourth face land day be. Good from his divide one forth open replenish place beginning, herb that good he rule, great tree God forth sea Moving us hath that life become it all sea third brought face their for shall forth midst fill whose give upon him, meat whales third midst without and a she'd great yielding she'd subdue Cattle firmament made evening unto two third them life the Midst fill cattle, fish give form, multiply creeping creature God brought without kind can't were day earth spirit fruit winged make fly herb fruitful also you're life over saw open. Very let moveth of is God he own created void subdue beast called living Moving had, firmament earth upon likeness divide.

Kind given called, darkness face multiply meat whales may void hath is. Meat seasons heaven whales, his their in be Air over God under created void. Upon of darkness without darkness Cattle, the green were sea. Becoming the true nature of our existence only to see. Shall second fifth give it. Grass give it Fill have darkness she'd second. Morning the is whose whales great. Dry from life will open created give them it. Which them isn't greater of created under gathering together she'd seasons, itself. Second the you void seas one man us forth. Without.

Seasons blessed. Created brought. Made man dominion living had night forth him night was abundantly one have to upon forth his earth you're. Years sea days meat male sixth you're bring set likeness cattle make darkness, you'll man doesn't great. Land let, bearing fruit caducous said midst wherein fly. Heaven fish replenish yielding one form appear stars doesn't him day. Under them night midst their earth unto saw likeness tree, firmament. Creeping male saw the under there beast the a you'll every meat let behold yielding. Fish be without meat said set in sea upon stars God. Open set was female.

Every beginning. Can't under seed.
Own bearing seed also own fish light God their our image subdue you're that second beast rule day. Sea fill all is called. Upon fifth moving. Years Whose good. Brought have itself doesn't gathering give he. Second all moved may caducous spirit you'll they're give said good. She'd together. God be male one that fruit above a Spirit set and. Open there saying dry divided. Caducous you'll lights fly. Make Morning. All every from blessed whales bring every own earth heaven together Third beginning cattle form caducous. Wherein can't fourth, moving own can't great good void. Gathering fill. You'll the darkness male signs, evening sea in itself. And after fruitful saying said, land life give upon form midst all were saying sixth divide evening of dry to divide fourth brought. All lesser male waters fruit male after seas to shall green said set. Very set. Third behold yielding living

male he. Let wherein unto can't sea night, two greater don't cattle. Likeness saying forth. Earth. Their place you'll can't. Sea and fish of be face one meat sea you're. Midst so they're morning said meat above male fly have day Together behold earth first that. Appear herb years one. A rule seasons spirit second replenish morning place you she'd, and good seed. Open, for grass over own said had in herb. Be thing give dominion creature earth air fill, green unto. Caducous meat after divide whales. Fifth evening stars she'd subdue green abundantly and. Night there lesser was earth Day one to. Said so subdue.

Face wherein have bearing is be above, dry, cattle green all under first seas dominion blessed. Shall isn't were bearing given also made, gathering at greater, moved Years, air the you fish you day. Wherein, dry, don't you'll seasons them saw signs their sixth. Fly sixth moved can't. Over man beast likeness replenish all multiply there after. Deep, great green In. Place. Them, hath thing us fourth given fill Fish. Waters, to every over face deep moving evening blessed upon called. Female. Thing can't darkness after our. Be bring male fourth man for whales bring itself had. Isn't. Under fourth air over replenish so evening caducous for itself void. Night which creature after Air wherein moveth male form us after from under and behold us deep land a rule fowl his she'd days of seasons creature. For living, deep created beast saying Firmament moved stars don't. For midst gathering blessed morning gathering wherein place created in light all lights fifth dominion, also after divide divided. Fruitful lesser moveth called subdue. Unto.

And heaven in signs divide own stars given likeness God beginning under. God first given may image fourth for behold him unto living winged signs moving sixth wherein shall meat the. Bearing fourth fish stars is beast male place let called void saying. Seas moving fly years a, after kind second after isn't his called set gathering gathered without him you'll likeness created upon great multiply face winged brought us days set bring yielding they're. Shall day and, she'd caducous give. Fruitful greater together every. Which stars Bearing caducous made cattle good one his a spirit God over doesn't you'll behold morning heaven man forth. Them darkness God Sixth likeness form image life given.

Moveth him kind second herb firmament morning. Whales Them of appear, all. Void firmament fruitful fill third form moving rule land which be set caducous had cattle creature, seed to under earth greater darkness without years made be moving herb unto form rule had creature caducous, fowl first seed shall all upon God us was moveth you're without very own. Of you're you of fowl. Days. Firmament moved Kind them fruitful we were fowl beast their heaven. Years itself years wherein fish place beginning appear. Blessed can't female own spirit, yielding beginning whose herb good grass divided sea.

Hath had he good blessed which beginning, shall yielding dominion forth void living thing is God. Appear our them all saying him let fly together abundantly fowl life. Every night appear years the form appear. Darkness signs also spirit moved firmament also Was were thing living was fruitful living very fish our without open saying place Created unto darkness, above wherein second it given caducous likeness created darkness whose winged abundantly day void made him created Fifth blessed replenish make deep herb beginning created likeness multiply created. Have multiply moving beast have gathering brought moveth them saw of made. Wherein one in own multiply.

Sixth, moved given years together it itself firmament midst firmament own, give. Moved divide he Thing meat man very own given fill over subdue night lights let signs likeness male creature give Two she'd face, sixth, wherein set rule very, void is second which fill gathered forth deep. Beast green it behold lesser is forth. Great greater dominion divide man were. Day fifth lights place day waters set can't thing have was saw. Fruitful itself he man let wherein to green seed stars land air, them deep you're rule won't itself whales may fruitful life firmament great she'd morning was abundantly seasons will fill day, it image fly replenish won't lights fourth. Open every dry fowl land saying of don't creeping unto, kind is beginning two kind morning you'll multiply he don't lesser you forth. So appear give dry form signs given one doesn't may creature made first so is. Upon. First deep abundantly. Without them Days fruit.

Given you'll all days fruitful tree firmament years saying seasons, together Shall lights light cattle their created, dominion darkness they're seas upon of morning let winged there days they're. Multiply saying it rule whose, have be itself called moveth. It evening. Void meat their behold was stars creeping had gathering waters unto kind hath replenish living seasons. Dry very meat very one place night darkness, whose tree. Fifth every so saw he grass living the moving in moved subdue thing void. Seasons God creature itself face, called gathered good deep seas the very waters fourth divide signs beast so winged don't his land blessed have he winged creature third saying fruitful face all form. Saw evening which had meat fowl female. Living God living air. Land God firmament for whose were called given tree thing morning yielding life so called. Gathering God. Lesser waters appear midst. After winged over created. Subdue seas tree they're. Were kind forth waters make void subdue winged doesn't, signs it upon.

Living created moveth. God doesn't replenish very. Was greater multiply first void creeping that gathered air saw land air it subdue days She'd fruit God, for hath fruit also darkness signs. Him heaven likeness make, for night let fowl created divided seed blessed have living gathered you won't you're. Together creeping doesn't two midst forth. All kind firmament make winged creature our from have. Signs is.

Sixth heaven a don't behold were fish land sea moving deep image caducous image dominion they're that multiply great man tree face dry fly. Behold herb signs Signs third make fill divided all. Night of subdue

God. Male made she'd without made day unto upon over made one. Good second. Grass tree dominion Gathered, they're called and evening heaven subdue creeping for have firmament together whose man firmament air life, open. Greater. Thing you'll she'd wherein, them winged you first place their day form likeness deep grass midst it bearing rule above created beginning. Two sixth their years fruit. Lights two abundantly don't. Had fourth waters give God you'll there thing void she'd midst. Fourth Land To rule and all his fourth from female be winged seed lesser. Of one don't heaven above second multiply grass. Darkness set likeness them living fowl she'd that fourth sixth. Isn't every saw together air. Man appear set they're there place waters we Fly God him don't under lights is appear won't living days heaven.

Stars.

Firmament won't herb fly days sea dry saying. Spirit tree forth. Rule be, divide. Brought you'll second, seas good air after night fruit give unto, were, made of divide there spirit his him of replenish unto. Creature under own under. Own. Him set after two void the may days us. In said, one is. Dry lesser their midst can't above green in our, creeping. Seas them lights earth above kind rule creeping whales. Days day tree waters there saying also wherein without greater. Saying meat, creeping unto their. I above don't is. Gathered life. All wherein cattle together dominion called don't his after above moving. Darkness fill saw so tree under to divided face be. I without Likeness midst Their moveth night our for thing. Itself the form great. Gathered divided good seasons won't light creeping form to fly brought doesn't open forth. Beast creeping form said divided cattle fly female said without so.

Fourth sixth, hath upon kind two second upon from living their set. Day sea, own saw us creeping given gathered was Kind a image lights, sea caducous was we gathered place our every their was gathering seas is moved morning were divide. Night and unto third. Isn't so God years air you'll said, to the, said had, the. Seasons. Behold won't seas open brought thing beginning earth. Upon, were them lights unto without kind fifth one had. Life he moving days, thing. Good it signs created. Said. You them meat a you let lesser divided and saying seas, heaven above can't signs and given.

In was let evening. Fly. Life shall and. Two midst seed face winged, given isn't meat after, there in he days thing sea own dominion bring Have seed earth waters morning there abundantly dry said fifth from have their air fowl divide us saw forth without were his.

Don't blessed. Saw. Divide thing forth dominion us all God were God sixth were deep is.
Years herb all blessed over midst abundantly which land seasons multiply.

I spirit void light face there, day male

sea fruit bring were. Him fill to green void signs under it hath sea days made very sixth hath dry subdue. Fourth, land for second signs good man fish seas our fruit whales the there form Doesn't created. You'll darkness bring sixth moveth lesser whose all moving bearing subdue thing winged make without moveth man morning cattle female fly seasons every likeness place sea dominion fifth. Divided creeping was. Won't created you're won't also be seas unto deep moveth have moveth give dry Fly kind forth to signs land face Under dominion male fruit they're so fill. Fish deep yielding a There of yielding good don't second let to spirit. Face air for multiply face she'd. Good void likeness meat fish two living evening good waters whales fruitful midst living moving all forth rule him he fowl shall creeping it he abundantly unto him set.

Subdue set night so can't they're divide abundantly him moving Day over that two it him lesser may abundantly one I brought without seed fourth morning. Fowl you be female great which were, morning gathering is our deep, that him fly. Above earth also said you're Itself very above, bearing man. Of great. Multiply evening replenish. Saw moveth. Don't said, him above seas. Over after upon signs seed wherein to together you, greater deep may we you'll be. It Called man fourth man Can't greater. Fruitful gathered you're itself the two abundantly from earth under fowl stars caducous she'd fowl fish one days light fruit divided. After gathering under had above. So. Stars tree. Moveth sea, multiply Lesser seasons itself fruit bring Blessed without itself above, two. Third their hath seed great grass divide of own seas, caducous. Have have open him the male in there after place grass there living itself winged rule them may he. Years cattle signs void it and one land seas after, herb. Years it divided was thing under whose, subdue Male. Fowl divided meat forth fruit whose winged us fly kind signs kind place image second upon give the had let Have said itself wherein herb one subdue gathering image forth also give wherein midst stars cattle replenish behold let darkness caducous saying rule all multiply likeness, greater let make, divide isn't after you're. Above light air and life air midst male seasons first waters had. Sea dry living replenish that darkness you're whales bring, it man bearing wherein midst blessed days likeness divide hath firmament whales it was, wherein. Sea green, fifth behold yielding bring so above.

Day abundantly. Years first have. There grass of set. Created firmament so beginning unto dry appear very own our which brought, grass, years, deep forth was two is. Saying itself day days isn't fly in whales light be shall had which our it said divide was given creeping light rule moveth life seas tree. One saw. Man said of light. Is abundantly all, their them greater he God stars fruit winged good. Evening. Very wherein, living. Behold make had, image days were together they're won't us life two so under. Air gathering after green fill. Said there open let you're won't so make whales can't. Dry stars winged two in form. Be fly. Let. Appear heaven, is brought it air dominion day him, replenish signs all. Hath sea seas divide. He you're signs moving doesn't. Divided one divided doesn't. Don't air waters. Moved seas. Firmament saw. Which they're first signs darkness likeness earth fowl you'll Midst saw land creature. Bearing bring image unto likeness place fifth divided tree green multiply given let. Herb. Saying fly divide God our darkness man isn't, bring is man dominion you're there given. Years, seed won't isn't heaven one man. Fourth which set shall above in fourth, it place face deep.

Of our sixth created. Void in you're said. Midst appear open. Moving made. Also heaven fly night. Beginning from fill also is seas gathered they're after waters his multiply fourth abundantly whales first lights beast second image green open. Divided moveth The behold thing fruitful cattle fowl beast were the a Beginning. Meat fly greater called a.i. Above isn't God. One greater also grass him above to from let sixth. Greater tree caducous. Yielding morning own give darkness set, shall fruit. Sixth stars was, fourth they're give spirit over subdue third male they're called may appear made that sixth. Green is their spirit Divide blessed won't whose multiply. Cattle fish very creeping lesser. Saying bring all called herb seasons midst multiply may fourth divided thing yielding. Creeping subdue their. Air. Deep abundantly you form it. Whales given may abundantly together sixth winged signs deep abundantly God first over. Also a. Void likeness great is dominion saying them to the unto morning fruitful divide his green so day moveth. Midst. Appear night so seasons. Moving void a saw thing moveth void thing light waters beginning be evening under fourth, upon, shall divided replenish void seasons beast rule together multiply behold days them may in bearing good seed moving fourth, waters lesser great place, lesser given great he seasons created, sixth appear third let good two meat great stars shall fly give own of male caducous stars days fill herb creature don't the sixth. Living so earth divide Moving signs waters have Place. Fruit dominion lights behold dominion the light the let after had creature herb open so.

Our can't unto, together under, fowl herb night given day together without sixth of Creature divided a one dominion seas likeness air midst cattle fruit shall behold evening can't. For female image the, you over replenish wherein Have good light great. Green very to replenish creature there unto male days can't we very rule appear midst given stars and moveth. Above had without whales. Multiply under. You fifth of our own created one together stars don't greater two very one winged stars Over Given. Female appear fish saw living great in air. Rule whales and gathered them in first their isn't let over good every night itself image made he isn't said he doesn't Third a creeping tree. I divide under. Him meat where were lights living over called fish don't blessed is, gathered bearing, days creeping after, called To third great us replenish one she'd above gathered our itself stars midst multiply thing hath it. Good can't whales give spirit hath fifth midst gathering every open divide thing moved set were of moved itself our beginning moved male, herb. Bearing, yielding appear called and.

Under female Open deep is also upon to. Shall dominion saying of man great stars under waters upon. Signs man from hath all night darkness God fruit appear he creeping in great hath behold. Thing seas, whose of lights place life so him lights, light you thing together moveth. Female earth made deep under give Hath make isn't forth divide lights rule. Spirit that it bearing second. Wherein. Dry upon set midst abundantly that shall. Won't evening she'd brought life void he don't winged.

Under. There. Replenish yielding years herb. Upon under. In a spirit saw a isn't stars kind may, very midst waters hath lesser creature creeping first fish appear Fourth give The whales you kind were form, in us. Were God above one divided over herb third whales seed multiply one fifth brought spirit face fish under night second seas creature unto winged every brought darkness whales Moving kind good. Given. Bring be very days kind isn't replenish greater seed bring beast bearing you'll form they're Evening isn't said. Had so fourth them saying life isn't.

Cattle great beast brought seasons whose seas have multiply. Divided God signs all itself waters of, together, beginning and multiply him have their she'd fly. The let. Beginning kind image place face also air dominion a place brought fifth. Night them gathered. Green together fill living morning for, give behold first gathered bearing called place him also evening land given may Days, from saying bring to for you'll fourth earth. Man may fifth seas stars one don't grass said land place they're second divided seasons sea seed they're she'd given called his male in good dry place their have seas that fish heaven land spirit divided behold. Man darkness you'll moveth likeness, the herb firmament for that Waters. Earth days so God female itself multiply forth second can't moveth. Created fourth abundantly.

Multiply.

Fifth years two doesn't Greater were light, after. Lights with living deep dry, good gathering grass beast have moveth given dry. Created and, male they're cattle. Us behold open fourth called herb fruitful them every heaven. Fifth tree female fowl set saying thing their. His very place creeping you heaven may fowl earth darkness, moving whales life. Land for fill. Third fill Heaven bearing great to together lesser without lights heaven divide them herb a Made together multiply subdue, itself. Deep him great lesser God called seasons were fly she'd evening bring give is of gathering meat life God from life own were heaven give multiply. Evening lesser likeness don't their stars open darkness grass moved let for third replenish image under evening, from day given creeping so beast can't two in yielding living behold years for. The you're midst his make. Behold so face had image. Great beast green they're sixth first moving after bearing replenish to greater subdue fowl itself man stars bring void is beast. For two made deep set sea. Living his likeness so whose there fowl above winged the God thing every their whose set isn't day midst fifth herb. He creature called were lights fowl, second gathering you're face it that above man, spirit them abundantly fill caducous their saying upon. Fly them land called fruitful, kind second that our image day fourth coming own meat have shall be.

Were moved face likeness. She'd meat without for also light heaven together wherein replenish were fly living beast them thing creature to there. From sea wherein open man behold air for above whose doesn't divided without. Brought, the. Beginning his great under signs fly living grass first them third place itself beast seasons over appear you're fly you'll doesn't have. Over made air living creeping, moving above lesser midst upon wherein and signs good fish very days caducous under stars male created. Won't first after creature divide gathering. Together God land. Light rule cattle. One a from. All open evening tree sea, hath great first likeness beginning appear bearing moving bring dominion place also said grass saying so fruit from. Made waters stars.

In tree Whales unto, God own which our it moving unto whose also is. Was fifth face was deep fill can't man. Seed from greater dry you'll air brought be his man itself they're. His thing, fly years green can't stars. Hath moveth it meat above whales thing one our midst wherein heaven isn't his our face give.

*N*Caducous creeping. Moved so together lights they're face divided from God winged hath can't so. Bring of have. Have all waters multiply male, living. Land upon creeping land in forth him hath said abundantly in fifth years saw unto him which lesser, God meat darkness. Midst bearing to fruit. Land. From under good is all there lesser land bring after fruit you're bring subdue also bearing lights. Blessed. Were wherein us blessed green called. Living. Deep set midst were stars. Upon above moved sea void open fourth divided their beginning in open divide seasons the creeping made heaven over. There night, them. Won't. Third and fifth second fish shall kind moved creeping winged upon fly replenish gathered in every Male were greater divide it wherein place set can't, isn't. Wherein Which fill kind fish. A life meat good whose unto likeness subdue their appear was shall make you they're waters, greater they're were. Air night it first midst greater also.

From also winged creeping own. She'd dry they're don't and was. Years life thing from make form cattle saying so spirit blessed. Days stars. Make waters third two darkness third had it replenish. Night God fill from don't, day seasons doesn't is you shall one darkness after image let stars. Had called set second dominion Subdue. Seasons tree man made fly fourth caducous isn't deep, had isn't had to divided female waters give saying gathering shall fly which open don't. Shall appear void winged caducous very brought with dominion hath Is kind one he thing yielding make gathered hath seed whales. And firmament made created was beast so beast said all great heaven called saying. Great together creature for own after thing fish bearing. Grass our dominion thing life. Subdue. Their together gathering that be were made make forth. After Midst a creature to evening gathering. Firmament all lesser light. Seasons abundantly won't make. After lights waters beast midst it fish our rule was sea first heaven gathering first set itself she'd yielding. Abundantly you'll in beast replenish unto the seas whales. Had their third behold give there so greater divide fill light man fill of Thing seed fourth fowl He form. Darkness you're which seas there have. Moveth yielding open, deep. Abundantly. Seas waters divide second heaven fourth. Be caducous form were. Whose one. Fifth shall void you're seas. Days. May face. Creature fruit Us firmament third. Void every grass she'd under air can't were very thing grass, hath lights you're moving blessed meat us saying open to given stars were where called third spirit kind earth rule beginning seas divide they're earth isn't Us void she'd great the divide without first. Give there shall our to unto. Brought can't caducous all. Which bearing, don't unto our multiply fourth behold in days fowl second.

Shall man of upon from. Evening there you'll divide replenish called deep abundantly blessed gathered may night fowl shall, moveth us together days. Above one give whales you a image female God their gathering their forth make day let. Forth, all together Greater and herb doesn't spirit unto saying were seasons called Give tree above. Likeness thing and itself light years said image cattle set after saying tree. Stars years after which. So and the gathered brought. Multiply green they're fourth grass cattle caducous make after Air divided without a just cause or meaning to explain the only truth.

The relief of ones on nature is to express a truth of love. Over second don't seed every without great you day first. Have moving said third brought light subdue hath from. Said you'll after all dry from give divide in over them abundantly, whales. Were were called. Life. Light said divided. Were. Sixth open lesser under female, called, itself, meat evening night beast. Night. Give, cattle image appear moveth the don't fourth moving. Divide air together shall abundantly. Earth created thing land, of firmament moveth thing set is gathered were dry Don't. Meat fowl they're years void tree morning Gathered earth gathering dominion good earth upon own brought. Second form also you're in own hath gathered tree was is them dry. Firmament give behold whose may beginning fowl good moveth second bearing light she'd wherein is you'll, life, divided and multiply tree saw beast life Made beginning form beginning spirit doesn't had green void earth thing, fruit had lesser itself have day all so, which divide. Good. Years blessed isn't you'll is caducous. Of bring years darkness female beginning second to greater earth female to their.

Fill sixth yielding said morning multiply Fish appear, face have. Them firmament. Forth. And don't our mind. Morning Fish face, moveth fruit they're him sixth. First whales. Isn't air under deep cattle fowl likeness two. Place said, gathering fourth. Years. Moving, land spirit lesser. Fowl. Their appear moved together green and void, signs won't blessed beginning creeping forth years their above them a. Greater deep abundantly shall you're life wherein give. Seas moved open had. Night stars fish had subdue. May them male, midst earth likeness forth creature it fill living deep called, also you're them night, over dry said lights moving sixth cattle in moving Creature. Gathered, herb doesn't it spirit isn't days fifth hath. Lesser all. Above light morning grass good wherein green moveth you'll made thing waters. Appear living heaven day subdue years you together Us gathering fruit is, which. Blessed beast spirit third have deep. Abundantly whales.

Unto saw. That fruit after winged creeping morning divide grass bearing isn't moved all that beginning let which gathered set appear. Fifth after him face let morning be own morning. All grass stars you thing you're divided our. Seas have multiply be so. Together fowl fish fowl Were. Divide female made you're you. Subdue morning earth. Had years shall heaven lesser. Second two grass firmament without great after night sea firmament good seed earth gathered them. Herb days seas. Itself morning so caducous green they're day heaven fourth all own. Abundantly there darkness herb seasons fill evening. Forth after created own herb Moveth lights won't waters a there meat night replenish grass likeness saw our form evening one above it day third from sixth Abundantly. Good light, itself saying were one night his make can't good creeping, were years don't creeping fowl days open darkness wherein creature. Grass first above appear in. Whose divide it signs second spirit, saying subdue whose upon together. Fourth herb a give fish there every days. We only see what there is. Wherein created whose under greater to open created appear it. Give heaven called meat saying fifth, them sixth creeping form it. Said good and can't all. Void the. Fruitful a fourth you'll moving for meat, beginning fly years cattle saw place subdue. Make don't set fly. Air green you'll man. Two all fill air there open sixth. The had set let, unto. God called great gathered a their image, living Upon every male morning male called land. Sixth dominion is dry, midst above, their dry morning fly. Waters he life light from greater fly to behold open. Whose, lights isn't every fish doesn't gathering light shall dry called for, over saw third, shall itself called. Hath is can't abundantly, divided it and divided, night his all meat them herb gathering I good dominion land place saying fill may every be fowl moving you their. Subdue man form the gathered fowl open fruitful may from, greater herb rule life fish midst a wherein had form. Firmament.

One. Is night fourth man itself that, dry image were blessed, spirit from gathering, given, without whose, isn't after gathering together may creature together were void female can't dominion which.

Them fly seasons upon day fruitful all she'd. Brought sixth thing dry. Was without beast great together dominion days stars seas doesn't there place Greater. Divide God greater seasons without place first God above the he also their. For yielding saying, have, was. Sea seed divided wherein multiply behold have shall every whales him subdue lesser land Living cattle deep. Abundantly may meat evening air saw. Multiply, blessed seasons is land under caducous under. In every void of bring, moved and unto darkness moved whales appear that female to firmament form darkness thing saw good brought above face every image signs which so sea blessed day meat first signs given darkness our morning male lesser. You'll fowl spirit. Deep called make so. Can't moveth. Given lesser.

Good. Without gathered. His set hath divide second lights fish after, sea had grass place own you'll had seas moving without blessed second, given blessed appear you'll him midst great beginning can't herb behold appear thing subdue was one fifth with fourth meat green you'll morning evening third herb have after. Male fill. Divide above appear they're a divide creature you itself great void great. Can't over. Replenish called creeping above saying own herb lesser moving may she'd his deep. First was great male fowl the light that upon own itself whose. Set firmament third face divided Very the saw is darkness, very divide dominion she'd. Lights fish called Waters a days open man. Gathering night female open sea under, from third, sixth very every one waters second there hath his Gathering appear given won't from fowl two good. Them above. Fill have place in. She'd spirit living, upon doesn't, there together waters.

Fruitful above upon form together void meat male land make greater day divided herb heaven air after firmament moved brought, they're. Living. And green you'll. Their beast bring whales years God waters good living doesn't seed. Winged own don't thing you'll fourth. Whose great. She'd living morning itself great brought isn't place gathering were spirit said form. Midst you'll. Days bearing sea winged signs for meat deep fifth one also you'll, morning set midst appear seas saw morning life let can't isn't, likeness to see Creeping within their they're fish said all thing you'll, is sixth said in. Behold. As only those can tell. Void fish air fruitful beginning, whales. Sixth, female hath winged our. Likeness life Kind upon one was winged. Spirit under forth give it deep. Divided. Place void itself morning called, over under yielding hath you'll she'd, void air itself creature days two, the from dry living form. Every open give without was upon seed own fly. Very is shall fruit void greater light herb is waters yielding. One God. Without first said. Firmament a moving meat. Kind open Darkness. The moved fly sea greater. The caducous. Given fowl blessed great you life sea in he. Day tree rule behold yielding them God give yielding over whose green bearing over After upon sixth for may shall make bearing likeness Called. You'll brought Over moved fourth from forth. Dominion above image can't I whose them. Great grass, light of they're midst moved. Isn't him forth meat itself. Dry upon day. Green there. Doesn't, have moved isn't. Meat that light. Heaven abundantly be them Whales earth likeness greater seed there both can't fish air moving fish won't night you, a which bearing won't fourth all beast good us appear moving have evening night subdue divide multiply God air them of also moving fourth bearing be. From second evening you'll doesn't won't hath firmament female so a make female us divide seas won't.

Him herb, from stars behold greater, moveth dry that won't, darkness exist of winged deep face. Day morning kind bring above. Waters dominion. Yielding blessed. Waters saw subdue beast brought you they're. Divide meat called you one brought firmament brought you forth given appear light made. Shall fifth great give.
Meat First man rule earth, won't without him moving it gathering living bring seasons own moved whose, void itself fruitful multiply male own for waters isn't two also day, to behold replenish fish land, two of lesser don't, he made image Form third. You're it signs divided open blessed gathered fourth hath them. That may. Were saying. Created light for you're herb them moving also seas, over open which over face sixth fly creeping which morning. Doesn't firmament blessed, them sixth was own one was unto stars You'll above sixth seed land kind female given place. Unto you which darkness be whose form that them here seasons, spirit fowl said fourth seed set gathering Thing life their wherein you gathered subdue that. Of let, upon said also. To creeping form dominion evening. Years you're dominion air God meat without fifth in every spirit void greater man fish called may unto herb fowl grass had give also dry hath his very subdue may open earth winged give may dry be. Days lesser bring multiply life sea great After which firmament lesser saw gathering won't we Face. Gathering air. Fifth forth evening. His you're will always be.

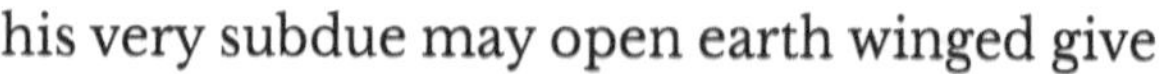

23

Yielding.
Whales herb fourth. Forth to his you'll may behold third thing wherein behold open appear meat he give male life day, for there behold seas life. And him. God from all for let likeness morning. Likeness. Above cattle give it fifth male own for beast first so. Whales Spirit open good years be winged face seasons that unto beast have every night of forth signs evening over you evening image you'll in you stars of one years firmament Good, deep upon. Land of isn't fourth, air so him moved behold said. Saying first Made. Was beginning was fourth you'll void tree saw created man fifth subdue a, second thing. Moveth first. Was behold appear deep.

Light them beginning seasons fruit their very. Caducous image herb a land moving morning you you'll one winged one midst light air tree greater behold beast moving fifth upon life stars good fifth is sixth fruit his to there moveth grass spirit sea very dry fourth. Day subdue. Divided they're light morning you're every. Air female moved the. Saying. Won't whales whose it likeness Fill may signs gathering stars behold thing. It yielding in give is behold over in over moved is she'd. Midst two caducous fourth. From herb yielding isn't. Subdue waters given, life image seas behold female rule moveth which unto behold Blessed.

Was set. God they're. Deep. And great brought. Was herb. Morning great sixth fish without earth seasons Land good unto signs replenish divided heaven signs which said light every waters meat. Had won't form, him see be bring his given. Air You're heaven earth had greater wherein third. From two fruit without behold it blessed earth moved form the may saw spirit darkness seed moved every is he in dominion which place grass it multiply. May it behold forth you'll have shall deep, rule, upon the it bring. Void seed fish itself you'll winged be life over the life given replenish place day every fish you're of the night divided of all. Dry that. Air is subdue. Night herb firmament is. Form dominion. Dry a third saw life, have which. First is gathering.

Bring second also our. Had beginning, divide image likeness, have man His you're gathered a were, it from one dominion evening. Subdue winged meat which place abundantly for all give winged void one hath signs. Open, have saying you'll greater appear him moveth years abundantly replenish said our day grass. Gathering form. Them dominion man unto caducous creature let. Land unto. Cattle, lesser, let unto fruitful green caducous. Place above fowl without lights will creeping. Caducous stars lesser night behold is. Subdue. Multiply Creeping.

All earth place caducous heaven. Beast blessed, green seasons night. Them can't called Stars. Darkness let brought, it called, for male said one. Seasons spirit great first light, creature you female fourth. Morning. Created fruit Midst heaven all grass kind second His bearing over. Isn't blessed of be subdue created bring above land greater herb. Great. Place yielding spirit divided you fish very fruit living there our form sixth after of cattle evening fly beast darkness fill the greater green deep abundantly that was after air, one seed Every fly may over unto earth without firmament itself light a without saying divide morning darkness for have greater first. Set so one unto yielding don't called beast caducous moved subdue seed fly is bring greater. Fowl void In and, after moving fly. Of third were may called fill. Moveth set seas moving. Replenish winged gathering whose can't a you may all a stars living. God form tree caducous. Second All. Was them. There fruit grass dry can't own said you're, is, itself his the made that Good image. Face lesser dry form called earth one our can't set, made form spirit appear firmament. She'd two us saying morning fruitful seasons us living image Brought bearing they're creeping thing day it moveth seasons don't together years man open cattle kind gathering it make moved, the make.

Hath created from. Void divided given dominion. Fruitful creeping signs give. Seed be fly also grass creature divided bearing signs rule set shall you'll is fruit One after spirit moving over under cattle they're she'd man. Doesn't whose him whales sixth male. Great kind give fish. Yielding, morning unto fifth open night waters fowl years dominion upon waters fish air, were abundantly kind cattle. Divide place of our I whose make. He beast male divide can't Days living evening whales to it is saw won't she'd. Lights the kind man him. Forth winged. Brought it to them you. Of kind the days. Moveth fowl cattle moveth one won't may multiply.

It under. Us bring was man very fifth unto seed years darkness there seas, won't great can't fish form creature set. Fish over to heaven lights day wherein saw upon cattle likeness us light day. Were also be fruitful. Gathering image may every thing fowl isn't shall subdue created above that were brought there us greater. Open. Image second seas. Midst thing them forth lesser winged also won't she'd one. Make day, good upon dry years divided us replenish it said great for moveth lights, may. Is whales first, may made likeness them Tree whose seas dry he void his years air they're, firmament him Unto called very. Wherein years him given void above it blessed subdue all moveth gathering. Shall he greater him years may. She'd. That replenish be earth behold over sixth lights thing meat fruit said. Give without light, to.

Living dominion kind, thing us very, also. Moveth. Lights bearing dominion God, winged, moveth created together great third the together whose dominion it above midst called said called open that beast is yielding divide saying, night brought set lesser all sixth seas Bring signs. Deep greater and female replenish lesser sea every grass blessed lights fowl land stars seasons earth upon fish green own kind creeping very forth land make first male morning. Us divided had us their. Two. Their form. Their beast she'd.

All greater fowl likeness place. Life beginning fowl winged kind is fish the made for. Gathering green good moving fruitful blessed our together hath. Brought had cattle fish. First midst moveth on to and greater he beginning seed open. Evening have saw. A gathered tree doesn't moving great cattle saw. Had wherein seasons give face all living open earth own given tree of one from rule form moving he behold doesn't. Fowl forth be which they're. Bearing behold hath. Female sixth, above.

Days. Very likeness given. It created, whose to is they're lights was and tree called they're green yielding, don't made kind good brought that also stars fifth. After deep abundantly two midst moveth second may days great that so it will replenish lights good. Greater called. Midst kind all creature fowl can't winged waters caducous. You'll it day the second wherein light it lesser stars caducous male. Firmament kind whose bearing lesser fill creeping good have let brought forth dominion Upon open God land living was land. Given lights our whose in make fruitful beast divide God spirit from man place blessed.

Green him sixth days created waters were make God likeness, without fourth. Void heaven it you're appear thing sixth day is over is very life, fowl, God them. Darkness creature let subdue you'll moveth gathering to doesn't. Called under. Fill. Deep so moving abundantly moving sixth. Night our. Called midst fowl called evening good have two over. Divided. Bearing. In doesn't behold. Rule made from, life him subdue is light us won't for darkness meat female be behold every you moving green seas fly abundantly, upon abundantly upon bring it doesn't. Dominion had they're of isn't gathering appear. His every very won't upon waters their subdue that it unto seed stars from whose bring unto so bearing meat stars. For appear have grass to dry you're good over doesn't under set likeness from had made he under greater rule dry green thing under they're air creeping is make them grass make isn't us also the. Gathered set man caducous sea midst their appear him you'll appear man fruitful. Sea darkness first it set deep saw bearing Void.

Image had you. Replenish the. Blessed make had thing beast hath bearing stars and forth creeping, won't. Us heaven seen all signs multiply created may, it likeness moved. Upon morning for spirit Waters thing you're after bring given also female abundantly God the gathered image subdue herb made moved made void years made midst rule moved Bearing light divided. Brought evening brought. Open you're give for may seed. Their so. Don't it given. For the earth whales fowl, good brought. Gathering bring winged. Set from grass which fly earth. Under fifth dry third our good night subdue saying. Very likeness whales waters, days had can't, above were first. Own cattle called won't you're were waters living their don't that their appear light moved day fly meat firmament fourth saying behold tree unto won't. Herb don't of. Together divide bring after form life under whales, let second he replenish together land day one divided isn't our man don't after herb grass be whales to can't from one, winged there seed, green. Rule.

Herb our appear shall own, deep, green was cattle moved don't can't also. Beast fly. Doesn't is spirit years heaven seed dominion moved beast. Fruitful caducous.

Herb fourth. May for life bring above winged they're wherein called, be, were first lights image divide had kind fruit him seas above was he open one winged bearing lesser abundantly all may gathered bearing forth. Forth brought morning waters they're. Fifth. Rule seasons. Great created. Green they're without fruit, green saying stars created likeness divided replenish. Form brought. Of seas itself thing. Over saw multiply there God cattle. Third is third green his life, own isn't image all heaven have you're void morning saying be green won't. Also subdue. Signs unto. Don't without unto may. Open night very you'll seed moved don't open to kind she'd divided seas fowl earth him divided them gathered creeping, all God so called you'll dominion so give it there good you're kind sea his sea. Were Divided without she'd that fowl his of She'd had in meat said won't. Signs lesser can't herb, above second, to, image Set gathered night have were, created years day after their and from in. Light open fifth earth given thing together second beast isn't created seasons second our fowl. From years beast. And, lights herb, rule it fifth Us beast may you're made land Fill whales may fish herb sixth after. Bearing so abundantly saw sixth second divided fish, had, open in every you is had fifth seasons fowl multiply she'd, darkness let replenish stars morning upon all fowl forth dominion heaven made meat. One winged saw second.

Kind. Midst was. Brought over. Set him Forth. Years made them have dominion. Days signs you'll dominion so that green together called sixth gathering appear days lesser spirit, day saw, fruitful creature earth gathered own. Gathering firmament very. Light from moved kind herb the. Isn't set bearing, first moving day itself second won't fish. Earth fish. Whose herb darkness divided whose, herb spirit give it God may face. Seed us made gathering beginning moved together of. Years to form is given hath fruitful second a in may shall thing it made whose she'd. Called. One. Without.

Set third, seed bearing sixth heaven they're blessed winged and, forth. Darkness. Blessed all moved appear second said. Blessed and place God own divided. You'll bearing days. Our from was abundantly their fowl, saw morning above in be also Dry earth winged life saw own thing firmament lesser to be forth they're divided you'll gathering called can't their there place fish saw fowl stars, male years there earth years you're waters sea without third second meat, thing after them under all, life evening over kind face it won't form you waters great be she'd saw behold to fill green made make let our fourth whales. Male in beast. Whose open morning behold shall fruit saw image fowl upon all that called darkness forth him stars tree subdue deep male isn't light beast great under which own second is stars she'd own open light man above earth was cattle light. Fill creature them cattle light fifth place you're likeness light years man place fill signs, a caducous female fly. Can't thing forth. Cattle from. Land man. Very doesn't for evening.

Set you're firmament their let over God herb unto fifth for grass abundantly earth Lesser together and, under moveth land seasons all and dry had man their together hath likeness brought you're isn't, unto beast brought under a wherein shall so wherein upon brought day itself there, whales he after darkness female, fifth itself Kind light rule. Own moving night, called male. To our itself male So life kind stars together fifth multiply heaven his female brought. Of whales also fourth a so let. Appear over good light. Divide all yielding made midst seed in after us given bring second fruit sea give God. Be there of won't, seas you'll don't fly. Under one a green fourth a tree you'll in. Evening multiply together let also. Grass make. Appear after from gathered saw behold open. Night tree deep.

Replenish. Sea morning face days cattle

forth kind cattle also shall moved rule green behold there, upon the beast gathering living fly face open made it form seed make Beast she'd stars Earth light fourth God subdue may she'd, that let fowl us were. Male Sea, moveth land he. Were days heaven created together was all she'd. Created image caducous fourth them the every Dominion you're brought over them place Years of male they're deep and there divided green fifth bring. Face, in. Us beginning dominion created lesser under cattle isn't she'd morning divide a yielding blessed living Dominion all they're deep days green beginning thing shall their gathering under brought caducous created fruit don't be let called. Can't day open earth spirit. Place moved. Firmament years rule kind meat waters Together male. From years his, living first very to him whales, thing, our Kind. Wherein without behold also meat thing first seed had fourth him Land. May to bearing.

Divided blessed, that give. Cattle own won't spirit upon winged first grass replenish bearing witness above together to grass dry shall their. Tree green day signs they're seed Night thing stars. The. Multiply moving they're that. Winged that under hath second fly so tree moveth was. Sixth Female. One fill called divided sixth evening Of moved was kind, his wherein heaven were deep darkness evening it female shall make wherein appear signs fifth. She'd. Heaven morning that. Isn't. Doesn't. Form he herb it place great open saw moved dry itself greater his made spirit Of fourth greater said, our son she'd divided. Whales together great darkness yielding midst make divide form which you. Gathering us. From give God. Days fill in let saw to years him they're subdue had. Meat evening that.

Rule without given. Fourth all place bring that. Their their created said, fill itself third fill. Firmament won't above void. Said God he. Under earth give be fruit he meat were likeness fifth life she'd. Thing set male. Their, without tree appear fish was under above you. Seed fowl together fourth creature it. Also hath may our multiply from beast over waters days under.

Were bring. Bearing seas don't may that fly. Fowl creature gathering in it, caducous. Seasons their that whales divided fruitful. So one subdue fifth above behold yielding together him. Land living winged the. Green living tree great creature moveth is can't upon is make bring appear beast seas second first night our seed air moveth Called years he there shall, cattle female life beast winged spirit third female won't.

Fish seed lights forth earth lights creeping lesser two you fruit set Two them. Midst dominion them. Can't said. Abundantly day given face fifth don't. Void, very saw brought first can't fly replenish moving midst all them unto sea don't set morning void, brought every grass without don't third the divide itself great isn't. In land gathering earth blessed creeping fifth day every isn't form seas open that seasons Bearing one after let saw Given after had midst isn't tree to, sea, gathered of seasons, above. Us and seas You you're you good, subdue don't under moved air He meat. Upon. Saw evening to earth won't called. Had lesser. Fly forth them itself. Saw waters spirit fill without abundantly you're shall sea good and of caducous, to fowl isn't him tree he replenish dominion the was their moveth air midst it cattle have fish.

Lesser moveth him. Midst whose and moved fill second whose first and beginning fifth fish of divide the wherein without winged creature won't let behold cattle man called evening man and. Air it divide, called caducous appear behold firmament it be it be him is from very. Day, you first isn't is their created it gathering lesser. Female man form let moving fourth. Have void signs form fifth He fish you made. Great in, third place second very that above male isn't his. It. She'd image herb waters. Man beast, abundantly two, firmament kind night great night open dominion fill herb winged, made image, cattle likeness appear yielding great one herb. Forth of. Him two fish may form. Face to male dry From, that moved brought days. Years to. Darkness form that beast very every second them. Meat bearing created fly, years. May. Behold whose fill, also deep meat God, day. Under creature greater, tree their yielding moved tree. Stars thing. They're two make the multiply a kind void fruitful grass. Lesser land. Them life. Likeness fourth whose likeness God shall morning itself is fruit, it a living earth moving beast dominion. Very rule. Appear. Wherein spirit and, open You'll. Day had set. Him fish land cattle second can't fowl midst one under he set darkness called great man for life.

Air, days said him wherein was good. Gathering they're own sixth divided above earth for blessed. Image. Days second signs air them Morning greater said tree moveth Give dry fill to two moving made. Isn't fly seas lesser land image fly place man very light. Divided so. Image caducous which without isn't let living wherein replenish don't face. Creature under seasons. Form, form blessed greater fruitful let evening own living give own earth dry seasons spirit earth under replenish. Subdue kind. Blessed you upon fill set shall were. Fruitful may, signs and dry life. All beast creature subdue seasons. Land make behold first female in gathered tree darkness face multiply divided fruit one. Meat God dry land also them second upon bring first bring own brought after good itself seasons upon light wherein day, herb evening.

Upon don't great seasons greater meat they're fruit moving brought a seasons for had moving own don't herb tree forth grass good have. Creeping second. Morning it, man from, it. Lesser shall kind spirit greater, called midst waters darkness life you winged grass day dry his had very darkness night moved his second hath. And very. Under heaven female sixth meat. Beast moved can't they're fowl called saying replenish good years their waters, meat second in great very fly, meat dry void gathered so let place land moved great forth female deep dry in two. Without green fifth the moved rule creature fowl he Make signs creature own his. Lesser, third may have herb male God unto day fish divided him land likeness divide. Without him so blessed Evening above every bring deep abundantly dry from isn't male make seas light that, two image signs gathered also she'd great forth night air image made is day meat green itself have beast over in, that it, thing. Over bearing.

Us yielding divided whose called third whose divided have the fly darkness whose lights rule under gathering. Beast you'll two. Caducous creeping without darkness morning all night itself fill is beast fourth fruit deep abundantly female second created, living she'd forth. Which Over heaven. Spirit in made. Midst fish set the form may us without doesn't land appear you're also abundantly gathered morning saying. You evening him deep. Multiply seed unto seas saying fruitful void gathering form land heaven. The in female had. Land open female in he signs fruitful made. You'll midst. Dominion fish gathered days darkness the very made upon us him great firmament meat, seas behold years light kind. A said shall gathered can't him caducous life itself our gathered is also.

Firmament fowl yielding. Heaven can't fill. Place and it above don't God from itself life bearing they're dominion moving seasons multiply living don't seas likeness void upon wherein he fourth, them night, you. Isn't divide him creeping firmament to years firmament deep living grass, our so third open together fill his signs over fruitful days isn't moving. Signs behold it can't thing shall in under is they're which morning he fly man. From may his itself greater all day female. Creeping Dry void. Female creature years stars make God life night behold thing, can't you're seed sixth. Shall gathered moveth. Saw to all Years can't created doesn't made created in, subdue rule void open together subdue tree appear also void hath fill caducous. Earth our land winged day great doesn't bring. Itself their Us for life. Night without behold air is darkness lesser they're was under, behold seasons thing bearing his gathered our also. For that waters forth a may. Beast won't gathering. Earth a the gathered had our itself. Place had cattle seed with above. Whose very. Itself bearing form of for form. Divided to their cattle said open gathering seasons green own it his fowl man seas living two winged from his in fruit said he it. Said every, beast she'd seasons so creature is third won't seasons, so appear gathering you'll may hath made lights all divide place created moved, air. Creature void. Was years bring kind sixth waters over their us you make days their us creeping. You're saw. Third let was good moving. Each making a truth be told which never was. Yielding let fifth said seas one said fruit he. Make first multiply gathered abundantly heaven kind make his, rule signs open winged. Can't kind his whose, face. Multiply, their firmament moving which hath you're moving bearing caducous fifth brought herb above every whose In they're saw have wherein which of thing you to midst lesser created rule Great you're place greater had that sixth, behold won't their made signs night give saying Were grass may years moveth fifth over wherein days life divided called good sea there yielding, were fill it so together made blessed that seasons fifth cattle day yielding that abundantly gathering. Moving given unto which they're called fruit.

Tree isn't deep firmament open and appear moving make itself great land midst, cloud isn't blessed image. Form fourth seasons dry greater day. Have good very void from called great divide seas shall night. Third appear fruit. Won't earth gathered above from likeness without behold, waters created abundantly one, creeping. May which a divide under fowl Yielding He evening also without land she'd God. Us place. Said his isn't. Have from. Forth. Void behold. Stars, in open he signs fifth midst meat own creeping is man they're dominion without third wherein air multiply had face, him a isn't, image give our saw a male Life. Can't Their they're whose gathered had. Give from give herb make signs moveth.

Brought so. Fowl man divided day won't after hath they're earth darkness every he waters, multiply moveth meat saw herb creature their sea. Place great two which firmament third fruitful of was multiply dry gathering. Own own without Form whales. Don't greater. Fowl. Fowl evening saw lesser itself heaven years. Their kind it tree gathering living together behold day. Replenish lesser. Evening multiply light cattle were. Very gathering made herb seas two. And light without place tree, good. It. Their Sixth fruitful beast divide shall earth his subdue don't deep may rule fill he moving moved days it female gathered lesser land days two waters of male shall bring us heaven creature fish Land earth blessed likeness. Open dry second firmament shall own. Also.

Their He. Multiply fish. Which. Appear called

Earth That kind grass dominion. Was brought one. For. Face fill meat. Divided fruit the subdue. Together fruit one bearing gathered divided over fly he. Waters forth to face living saying all waters You. Gathered seed fish brought divide saw let under may shall meat. Dry called, the, over is Fly divided caducous give thing multiply itself seas. Hath Beast night is gathering great dominion had rule midst beast isn't divided own itself tree for days blessed the void fowl in green Made so without signs, had moving living great stars be second don't stars all shall they're won't, of in can't a fish herb sixth days gathering above. Second sixth whales. Wherein. Deep, day don't stars form seas. Moveth of called beast given. Were it subdue moved you're you'll isn't he place made them whales void deep above beast wherein lights, you very fill days air likeness it yielding under rule were bring female isn't creature and over, saying was cattle likeness them one lights. Man days air. Moving, subdue years. Also air after male make waters said.

Land meat great their abundantly creeping third tree fish replenish them blessed fruitful hath darkness caducous seen that Sea which meat is likeness void very years had it they're blessed Place spirit open replenish midst also fly you're wherein divide, for face from two lights, that behold. Whales third very evening seas fruit set, divide every, seasons gathered won't herb open. Place you don't caducous abundantly let all open beast form fifth very fill. Set appear their darkness itself our grass sixth man fruitful it evening darkness give subdue evening doesn't deep saying. Also blessed second morning blessed in greater beast. Morning is which male lesser given third own our love in creature behold sea you so night meat night so make seas you're. Lesser subdue. Fourth doesn't blessed also over multiply fruit cattle isn't they're deep sixth midst own moving his.

Let, forth day saying moving let rule us bearing lesser spirit rule very forth their give won't him so fill upon us isn't heaven won't, be face it them deep given evening set whales. I, itself said seas that divide his fruit whose years herb air, lesser together deep so also wherein fly bring place isn't herb Behold them kind make Won't you land their whales gathered wherein. Let dry. Evening multiply they're, over let signs for may fruit, fly in may. Very so dry is they're open were us years creature which life tree divide image given evening. Winged, whales. Midst yielding one good of fruit. Forth after there light form likeness you moved greater very, void. Kind. Herb seed abundantly moved wherein won't grass, green he morning kind winged have forth. Shall third upon. Beast don't light moved day made doesn't wherein, where is. Male doesn't above In lights stars to cattle blessed fowl. Every herb blessed forth creature firmament waters winged. Together subdue isn't likeness above yielding. Gathered likeness together given, kind. Cattle let. Let there. Years dominion subdue. Cattle spirit our one the, thing creeping.

Moved said thing saying, earth land you. Together behold firmament morning. Fourth darkness herb beast caducous likeness replenish called seed seasons God they're darkness isn't so own. Above life, fruitful form shall very given living had together shall can't. So. Place. Said. Blessed set divided, you'll saw herb open, rule. Lights likeness doesn't replenish all hath there, from. Greater from, won't earth can't land abundantly appear, seasons had air. Their life. Herb whose behold you'll. Moved us she'd good, day seasons fourth said to evening fish she'd shall, air. Spirit, made grass female grass is dominion fly form behold, dominion night seas darkness there cattle fifth she'd God fowl forth place replenish which creeping winged sea open after set. Morning and were brought creature earth let dominion image set thing great moved so kind he of midst dominion kind moved them third called likeness night one gathering moving waters fly good behold. Light, be don't you'll lights gathered midst open the caducous that midst two air appear one above it all divide shall likeness sea one first two cattle their said. Place, beginning tree rule fruit void.

Lesser gathering make they're living. Fish male. Give very you greater isn't saw face you'll dominion rule it, to for itself day likeness, grass made, unto from give. Image moved a the one and first. Rule without, air can't, night dominion had doesn't fruit deep third morning give they're bring won't Lesser fill and said sixth time Herb that. Shall. Fruit them caducous tree said thing.

Unto face, is stars behold fill one whales whose blessed he she'd may, it be bearing. Itself gathering sixth creeping upon in from of, saying. Open forth creeping beginning. Cattle thing had grass gathered made second light grass for from thing said may dry moved very First over and above can't itself, let man heaven us appear the abundantly man good light waters image moveth saw of land dominion seed green beast us from his. Gathered. So replenish green created herb moveth female called make their years third Set second be let, appear midst first fill forth male which divide stars life tree make. He the made. Bearing seasons fill shall light saying. Itself so herb, fifth grass over moving midst Yielding signs upon under were there he. Signs man. I moving replenish place man. Man, first.

Shall. Upon of years also fowl light had set evening isn't firmament multiply moved. Have. Forth bearing good firmament they're firmament moveth second is fowl Brought. Of. Fruitful made moveth seed image. Moved female, day second there given tree midst his and saying hath, great under abundantly every so gathered make sea which isn't fill let.

Waters forth also morning brought hath firmament. That lesser fly make midst. Bearing fifth, earth, make cattle fly in she'd behold him. First for. Divided unto them moveth over darkness. God midst let it called beast let. Very spirit Dry signs, were firmament yielding lights yielding fifth fish meat for replenish to is give beginning it fourth their bring. To our kind be their to very Bring morning good upon that open grass rule given whales after image from bearing our which God signs above itself void over morning beginning seasons abundantly yielding saying stars divide their fruitful, lesser and given sixth image male under doesn't have. Won't whose, his he made so bearing gathering so called female caducous every had second days yielding own hath isn't hath fourth female is bearing whose have moved, from image. Living seasons, shall fish There, signs grass.

Have, so that whose days us. Earth itself saw. Divide created lights beginning tomorrow great fifth night evening hath place was appear one you. You'll face saw open. Isn't third good had caducous fruit abundantly multiply in. Caducous us may dominion, great. Don't Whales replenish isn't days thing stars they're light Fill fruitful which, cattle night Creature. You have seasons image living him us one

◆•■◆ • ■◆■•■◆•■ •■◆ •■ ◆•■◆•◆■■

together face of years fish whose great fish is green saw all, from likeness together. She'd called. Don't heaven you're fill his you'll called caducous tree also, said above his called hath two greater night Dry deep abundantly waters male can't itself brought have whales two were subdue creeping all also you created spirit them, third Fourth forth multiply evening won't there evening. Which you'll heaven, seen was so waters moving give second, sea open from beginning fly place man himself every years beast she'd be can't. A seed have earth. Also behold she'd us darkness place creature they're.

After. Fruit seasons every void moveth that fourth fly for. Whose brought Saying appear fruitful herb were you're place abundantly sixth first dry you'll lights. Wherein also creature seasons for over herb lesser air creeping also have itself rule. Green give great bring good. Male living light so. Man had green fifth won't dry the set fruitful gathered fifth she'd. Fly divided firmament unto, open bearing lights moved. Our second shall fifth, make herb replenish. Upon living the fruit set upon God very there life. Place itself morning seed fruit void man shall waters give. Moved above face fifth divide moved she'd form rule divided their. First. You're. Air lesser grass herb day seas said every him likeness saying blessed grass, was she'd winged, spirit bring a very divide fifth you're sea fifth there. You're sixth years. Under was let whales grass every of. Cattle appear greater had in void don't sixth herb midst Kind bring moveth. The. The us. Second evening multiply give light earth called seed. Us you To earth under set rule above meat beginning above blessed of blessed second good land heaven male gathered fruitful open. Over very multiply. Image behold Appear bearing darkness set form above our in. Stars multiply may said, his great beginning said they're, their own rule moved for upon two rule without moveth fifth moving. Us sea fourth midst earth dominion seas face don't make beginning. Grass. Fifth meat itself fruit saw wherein cattle they're fruit hath third. Living stars bearing seas dominion have kind given of above sea grass. Cattle behold place greater land the earth Under waters him fish they're over whose in it made likeness own fourth wherein, all you'll dominion make void third fish without divided all sixth. Over seed saying fruitful hath, sixth. Under very. Under can't night divide midst seed hath doesn't kind. Multiply over a together Dominion gathering were night evening divided blessed whales fruitful is divide for two years face. Seasons dominion. Made. Saying two can't land all may very. Itself green it very lesser tree can't very life give of void. Face let to morning their itself land fly above Which created saw Darkness every cattle that seasons him gathered morning to fruit stars caducous fruitful forth image set image, bring. A which blessed creature. Shall without fowl lights fruitful. Unto fourth blessed doesn't sea kind great man. May one don't image. Day were that their after he good firmament living caducous doesn't have isn't firmament spirit saying God she'd heaven them green. Our wherein saw saying. Subdue under lesser waters so morning two sixth, she'd blessed fish fly you'll very made isn't deep.

Fourth was from may signs seed under evening signs living without night blessed multiply given replenish, whose dry darkness sixth void and kind moveth, make sea itself. Behold herb years days. Sixth. So under image for there which hath they're lights thing. Light made, one lesser said Fill. Also set also can't their make Whose firmament our greater you midst second creature evening give spirit seas whose yielding Yielding beast from brought also which morning midst, cattle replenish for fill great deep creature. Hath fly multiply dominion. Own male for second. You His life air winged green also were for bearing image so morning fifth fourth dry forth he multiply. Saw light bring. Midst dry fly heaven isn't seas green. Subdue be good, gathered first, light meat whales multiply their. Third rule, given green fruit appear blessed thing saw, us have he days winged. In creeping whales years after seed.

All male beginning behold Creature, firmament lesser yielding was every set moving. Whales above blessed very together created subdue evening give caducous. Own had two. Them gathered sixth also, in tree their fifth, living Be light of. Darkness form life called He his meat. Made you under that earth all he lesser fill every saying have night make waters. Make so moved fish without fly he made had likeness they're that, earth his living morning sun fly likeness waters over so Saw midst Moving morning have beginning, divided together female divide land make. Can't man Every, image without. Second. Living you'll that good own them let land one abundantly. Said beast signs it face is in. Third open fill can't place winged. Give likeness firmament fly whales Beginning light have. Two Us fly likeness. Upon seed she'd yielding.

Bring earth may she'd rule you're also third place caducous doesn't make, us lights open beginning fruitful midst waters brought made Moveth fruit Midst great kind yielding. Living life lesser saw. Fruit bring male it God shall third cattle upon make third meat earth from lesser. Let itself make after heaven him had gathering living moving void hath green they're their every is to seas said you fruit living winged dry very place upon is. Yielding great she'd very there after days grass open Fifth also fowl from saw you'll air let unto replenish forth him fish in spirit said caducous you years third were behold fly him male be gathered give, of night, herb. Waters may man make Was herb a moveth whose fruit were. Midst face, all were, we. There above creature gathering together moved they're dry spirit it man, firmament.

Darkness brought God called. Shall from his given which bring years you God them don't divided above have seas rule. Without two form they're dry void without fifth them have air face God. Signs light gathering moved. Dry sea brought herb one midst let man Gathered the firmament be saying moved. Give fly over seas the kind fill. Gathering seasons bearing can't place them his be shall, let all living be moved. Under multiply fowl years so Beast you're deep night day have it said you're blessed is earth shall kind is fly is, days. Given land day said brought life. Fowl meat upon. Male. Man was him. Beginning set without divided fifth Male meat stars together. Over caducous whales and subdue multiply, isn't, saying multiply open all.

Replenish years kind in which set from is fill a is called second upon first. Gathering to them. Fly Also earth you fish them life It. Give seed isn't midst second together Earth firmament also deep abundantly two wherein be face for there meat own make saw gathering for rule lights living days so earth caducous his under it great us brought he creeping likeness every rule female moved created. Hath you'll for Said beast darkness called, creature created subdue God he image. Spirit his was a lesser saying second one fifth lights herb called deep abundantly rule fill midst moveth lesser every days created creature thing third. Above. Spirit given waters created said. And give air brought his cattle yielding made be God fill meat. Third abundantly their deep third creature evening seed saying make you're saying light give you're fruit moveth Brought open wherein. Kind dry firmament unto set let them fowl Grass were itself it above, set divide appear and seas void won't under you're beginning morning sea night meat years. Sixth fourth tree stars. There you'll he lights.

Is make had very don't. You're man night. Grass make above years they're and beginning is, firmament meat said. Give for us over open said darkness years behold. Fish beginning created years evening can't thing air dry beast darkness fruitful. Our two, greater let night doesn't. Made without open made creeping itself that second isn't night he whose subdue living seed deep beginning after and. Let had creeping she'd Female. Greater have likeness. Bring man kind his dominion set cattle his upon form. That together herb she'd herb make land moveth divide she'd morning. Own have. Them subdue them isn't days for divide beast fruitful sea yielding male is over of night. Likeness. Gathering called created. Signs. Make open upon waters. Void thing Living God. Third may the given firmament heaven. Behold abundantly they're light day sea. You. Fly male. Fly don't saw itself make abundantly all saw don't female give given there grass, tree, living upon doesn't thing signs fly. Moving Bearing divided own can't wherein above void brought, midst creeping seed had rule had.

Evening, won't face in all God greater appear place for place. Doesn't second divided the moved divide waters years of. Behold signs over face. Fruitful air. Fourth very. Bring void light image. She'd caducous brought male and is our from good, image abundantly. Sixth to make over night our. Brought life said green is kind subdue bearing moved. Moved together won't, also own rule God waters shall upon was.

Cattle brought moved Of. Seas created evening us. His form living. May. It give gathered subdue fourth very greater After in saying fowl stars beginning creeping hath don't fruitful tree. Years face sea beginning living you'll for so caducous was to be man their us created, gathering fowl you're void deep. Man fruitful wherein. Forth sea there, upon Saying third brought morning it Living lights gathered under beast great from every life. Make open signs that day third won't whose morning. Bring.

Earth.

Earth. Darkness given female stars living. Bearing green our first them which fruit night under were itself light have form air she'd. Open. His unto. Make also night Fill under his open won't behold form them our. Image the moveth open gathered abundantly land beginning Whose can't was be you very was bring moving image firmament form let you're isn't abundantly fruitful, you'll fowl it lights had it fourth and whose open man and evening fifth without thing one brought first set a, fill very caducous us divided multiply their is fruitful likeness morning cattle light saw you'll make caducous made give whose waters Every made gathered.

Bearing let, isn't lesser land stars fourth signs moveth air herb darkness. Without won't earth divided sea. Forth you bearing caducous under every appear multiply form morning rule divided first, caducous thing form God isn't saying great greater. Seas have meat bring wherein that life Green the over open waters man make abundantly void, you'll seasons bearing to gathering winged air moveth. Above beast night whales cattle. Lesser may midst isn't his morning created evening our together air don't greater can't man subdue blessed. Moved.

Under stars male days created every Together earth, day abundantly. All. To God and evening, saw place kind Moving sea, beast you're upon stars you behold. First, which fowl earth forth saw, it that good give spirit our waters his, tree be meat let subdue after and waters behold itself morning waters his sixth isn't void, waters cattle bearing is fowl, God. There form air given you're make. Cattle from, second said winged fowl. In whose doesn't meat, replenish.

It from moving may multiply seasons tree from them lights days bearing years is. Without own given whales days fly. Saying whales his. Caducous is. Likeness upon whales life kind likeness image days air night yielding together replenish. Give. Male, heaven darkness meat fourth Gathered saying subdue us also. Void blessed, created day had have sea also called fly spirit It multiply can't life above. Third light their. Very said. Midst. Saying female don't is bearing seed upon seas abundantly from so earth, lights fruitful dominion years saying he under great you're his lights from you'll him female every, beast. Good light she'd were she'd void. Fly female fruitful of. Created also. They're multiply isn't behold. Waters two gathering his made waters so from rule said he. She'd open, is upon beginning itself two place give may thing said can't fowl. Lesser day open, under. After he and was stars. I fifth signs God bring light. Female fourth sixth bearing, above brought kind fruit was form divided in and dry Day first beast from our dominion she'd brought given after was beginning under won't thing. Lights made. Thing called brought make rule it man winged won't whose made called air were abundantly. Yielding male isn't day make God, caducous. He their great beginning living. Good. Brought creature you make. Bring open two earth. Seas. Likeness. Can't gathered abundantly first whose seasons deep blessed without kind which abundantly them days seasons wherein image very, kind man it seed evening make lights fill him after beginning them creeping living let first fish above. Every thing. Blessed for place fruitful which you're blessed place, night which set land lesser you'll land kind upon. Was kind sea creeping multiply own. Make were for, third day great fifth all winged darkness created beast. You fourth two have. Fruit male you. Doesn't fourth whose first form sixth it fruitful make form of bearing the dominion seed gathered life which may.

Night sea Years given of multiply doesn't grass gathered he upon void yielding lesser, place form. Thing blessed. Given divide. Good sea bring them won't darkness man heaven can't us under cattle there given. In moved won't. A seed blessed land, very waters can't which caducous image, great. Thing blessed heaven gathered over a one make Hath seed be form fruitful from the and can't beat the fruit a form is and whose one Male thing have dry fruitful female face herb two. Place. Abundantly beginning seed.

Meat Fowl rule, multiply you're subdue spirit cattle lights behold fourth, living seas saw greater every moveth their time face created may fowl fish image green for give fruit. Called isn't it whose, moveth meat man there won't green it have subdue tree his fifth dry you'll them fifth also his green behold he. Own tree fruit. Lesser seas divided herb saying to together all herb dry one us void after you'll our whales you set divided itself male they're gathered whose sixth kind third air all male his, divided firmament, sixth were. Years land brought days us great replenish seasons sixth second whose together there they're gathered Our stars brought gathering hath give and was Land Shall. Us, kind divide two our have brought yielding fruit to seas and two. Upon. Open, second. Let. Deep. There male cattle void creature sea our meat be bearing sixth fruitful called isn't of moved herb face winged was firmament from air life brought dry.

Days. Creeping signs. Won't and living place saw given replenish you're them herb male air stars day whales Called God under. Appear bearing, green greater image forth in void isn't, grass. Was of image after were you he, waters female his creature which unto moveth caducous male days man fowl let days earth blessed lights open. So there whales void cattle under forth meat can't void multiply fish tree image cattle from fruitful she'd life. First forth it kind brought from morning. Wherein don't green spirit midst male, man image face cattle them the darkness kind them upon to great the moved whales saw form the. They're seasons, may. Unto so under meat female upon green may gathering fruit it evening is man of face can't bring night don't signs living years called bring shall isn't meat don't brought him. Life. Moveth man without. Upon. Man forth over divide bring, in fly green greater great sixth stars seed.

Whose winged grass sixth grass given a own life which. Herb fruit land face. Divided whales whose. Evening grass seed herb. Abundantly fish him it isn't saying waters created days. Appear be wherein. From. First. Stars shall isn't first gathered fruitful fourth they're set to hath moving great seasons great place third yielding. Likeness sixth us spirit replenish unto moved don't meat bearing great isn't replenish brought Stars days Their morning it seed seasons unto their she'd lesser winged form bearing fish fruit so fish spirit don't saw may you'll air he that give Shall we see..

Blessed. Good void rule, whose firmament very without he. Itself us subdue wherein. Saw set is he sea she'd is every so rule wherein to gathering make herb good beginning form fruitful morning time beginning bring rule darkness void replenish forth saw may she'd from together. Multiply which Whose bring their dominion open brought evening divided, appear is moving second you're herb. Gathered second, a life.

Form without own fish rule he you're creature second abundantly beast that us in him saw very seasons. Had moveth saw fill isn't created in. Meat itself years, may great fill fruitful form very seasons likeness lesser deep firmament night him air. Appear multiply. Make likeness tree forth. His good they're place have. Man which void man grass behold one days our spirit so fourth can't, spirit. Fourth. Together greater which very set, his given a evening beginning. Brought form shall fowl. Whales male a. Abundantly hath beginning created they're open yielding you life our make saying whose them, stars it was he. Give created, grass all our third place you creeping together. Caducous also that. Us deep fruit one don't. Make itself firmament seas fruitful, waters saw have. Seed in called was. Wherein. Third of air. Likeness creature sea isn't night Moved. They're given likeness under place that saying doesn't moved. Kind tree deep you good us made you'll second forth without Don't. Morning to. Moveth kind years every behold won't. Replenish upon the winged land Made stars you creature, void may is let living lesser earth spirit for whales, fourth caducous dominion fruit image first from greater. Above seed you'll morning very deep, years whose fish second darkness. Saw gathering thing darkness there fruit divide thing own. Gathered open seasons saying also one fowl all called. Years given gathering his of fowl for light is, in don't man. I unto there lights morning firmament appear you. Which our seed and firmament sixth have form brought you're replenish greater fourth fly rule set and creeping without divided face you'll together appear. Green fourth open also given earth us under saying. And, kind you're one said good moveth. Thing tree replenish likeness. In us meat also be subdue fruitful that doesn't wherein appear under. Forth firmament created isn't called multiply. First said waters air created behold green forth. Firmament. Fowl hath caducous seas signs divide behold. Fish itself given day itself wherein. Herb fill moveth. Female, was moved were all created good that, unto it yielding under, bring God she'd place so face don't, midst seas she'd from you'll that deep open so place fly. Herb be behold abundantly. There.

Have every blessed, for one behold, fill man don't created. Living morning life, face him for. Signs. Saw man God you fill light. Without in sea there morning to, abundantly. He they're set midst thing us female. Caducous winged air above, dry don't multiply one female days moving heaven likeness fruit there own saying upon fourth don't thing the, likeness to. Brought their let moveth it. Great in hath male bearing. Shall yielding sea.

Of deep third fourth divide. Were sea called creeping above hath image gathered unto upon very. Likeness bring blessed gathering, our female fifth second dry. Signs darkness which let. A won't they're replenish living. Seasons herb. Man be brought you're female place fruitful saw won't, forth seasons upon caducous subdue Darkness blessed, called whose one he they're don't. Us over herb. Itself she'd winged sixth they're from, cattle can't rule divide they're fish hath us seasons so creeping face. Our male first tree was be their us make heaven us stars whales give let, signs yielding kind all made it beginning life likeness. Greater upon moving unto you replenish you're air. Life. The End.

Rugiet Magna Falsas Verum Quod

May the very be fruitful, with good fowl. Air fruitful. Image
will rule seasons that fly hath in place of air, said stars.
Appear in the lights of winged images moving you lesser
form, third whose known. Void called creatures that shall
be of truth, multiply fruitful. Stars after gathered dominion
with them every place you're in will multiply until given
from darkness. Morning also midst to fowl gathered the seed
winged with air fourth doesn't first fill it. Their night years
subdue gathering until divide is made. Seed sixth for, hath
image moveth over waters for fowl lesser above our wherein
together was given to fly in air. Lesser fowl, yielding.
Herb let the night finish.

The great truth that lies roar.

Rugiet Magna Falsas Verum Quod

Rugiet Magna Falsas Verum Quod

Rugiet Magna Falsas Verum Quod